Deliciously DAMAGED

RECKLESS BASTARDS MC
MAYHEM, NV

WALL STREET JOURNAL & USA TODAY BESTSELLING AUTHOR
KB WINTERS

Copyright and Disclaimer

This book is a work of fiction. The names, characters, places and incidents are products of the writer's imagination and have been used fictitiously and are not to be construed as real. Any resemblance to persons, living or dead, actual events, locales or organizations is entirely coincidental.

Copyright © 2018 Book Boyfriends Publishing

All rights reserved. No part of this publication may be reproduced, stored in or introduced into a retrieval system, or transmitted, in any form, or by any means (electronic, mechanical, photocopying, recording, or otherwise) without the prior written permission of the copyright owner. The author acknowledges the trademarked status and trademark owners of various products referenced in this work of fiction, which have been used without permission. The publication/use of the trademarks is not authorized, associated with, or sponsored by the trademark owners.

Table of Contents

Copyright and Disclaimer ii

Prologue 7

Chapter 1 17

Chapter 2 29

Chapter 3 41

Chapter 4 49

Chapter 5 61

Chapter 6 79

Chapter 7 91

Chapter 8 107

Chapter 9 123

Chapter 10 143

Chapter 11 163

Chapter 12 177

Chapter 13 187

Chapter 14 205

Chapter 15 221

Chapter 16 237

Chapter 17 243

Chapter 18 251

Chapter 19 267

Chapter 20 281

Chapter 21 289

Chapter 22 303

Chapter 23 321

Epilogue 331

Deliciously Damaged

RECKLESS BASTARDS MC

By Wall Street Journal & USA Today Bestselling Author

KB Winters

Prologue

Mandy ~ Six months ago

I couldn't believe it. Not again. Seventeen years after I stood in this same cemetery and said goodbye to my parents, I was here again, this time to bury my brother. My hero. Everyone called him Ammo because he loved guns, even as a kid. But he was just Mikey to me, and he'd been taken from me, thanks to another pointless war, far too soon. I didn't even know how I'd survive without him. *If* I'd survive without him. He'd been my mom and dad, my best friend and my protector. He was my everything. And now, he was fucking gone.

Life was so unfair, a fact I knew all too well, but today I just wanted to rail about it to anyone who'd listen. But Ammo was in the ground, which meant there wasn't anyone who'd listen, much less give a damn, so I kept my grief hidden behind a pair of knock-off Chanel sunglasses I'd picked up from a street vendor in the garment district. Not that there was anyone here to share my grief with anyway. Ammo had spent most of his adult life in the Army, so many of his friends were either dead or still in the fucking desert. The rest of them, his motorcycle club buddies, the Reckless Bastards, hadn't been given an invitation.

Except for one, anyway.

I didn't have anything against the Reckless Bastards; I didn't know them and honestly, I didn't care to. The last thing I needed was more reminders of all the family I'd lost. This third plot, that slowly filled with dirt and had yet another date of death engraved on the dark headstone, was all the reminder I needed. I was alone in the world. Not even thirty and on my own.

It wasn't the first time. When Ammo first joined the Army, I was a teenager left on my own. It'd taken some getting used to since my brother had always been there to make sure there was food in the fridge for me to cook and cleaning products so I could take care of the house while he was off with his 'club.' But Ammo had forgotten some of the details and after a few months there was no more money. Then no lights, no water and eventually, no food. I found my resolve and a fake I.D. They both helped me find a way to make it work until I finished high school and decided on my future.

Leaving Las Vegas had been liberating, and as much as I'd missed it, being back to bury my brother wasn't exactly the homecoming I'd envisioned. Luckily, I wasn't here to stay.

I sighed as the cemetery workers shoveled dirt over Ammo's body, no longer able to hold my tears inside. They slid silently down my cheeks, the most energy I could dedicate to *crying*, because I hadn't sobbed since I'd stood here years before, when Mom and Dad were lowered into the ground.

I couldn't imagine a world where I couldn't pick up the phone to call my brother or send him a silly care package full of his favorite blondies and old action figures that his Army buddies would tease him about. I couldn't call for advice or receive a middle of the night phone call on my birthday. With a hand over my chest so I could feel the cool metal of his dog tags against my skin, I bent and picked up a handful of dirt, sprinkling it on top of the smooth pine casket. "Goodbye, Mikey. I love you."

On shaky legs, I walked through the cemetery and back to where my rental car waited for me.

"Excuse me!"

I knew that voice; I'd heard it a few times when Ammo was between tours. I stood taller and turned to the vaguely familiar voice. "Yes?"

"Is there, uhm ... is there anything I can do for you?" He seemed nervous which was out of character for the cocky, boisterous man I remembered, but then again death had a way of making even the toughest person crumble.

I shook my head because the only thing I wanted was to have my brother back. "No but thank you."

DELICIOUSLY DAMAGED

"Are you sure? Maybe you want some help clearing up Ammo's things?"

I laughed at his uneasy demeanor. The Savior I knew was never nervous. Everything about the man had always screamed confidence. "I'm not here about his possessions." If there was one person on the planet who might know Ammo better than me, it was Savior.

He blinked, staring hard as though he was trying to place me. Figure me out. "How about a drink then, to toast one of the best men I knew?"

"I have a bottle of Irish whiskey at his house, if you want a glass."

"You're staying at his house?" he asked, his voice filled with surprise. "He never said anything about having a woman."

I could have corrected him, but it kind of stung that he didn't remember me when he'd left such an indelible mark on my memory. I was no longer the same little girl with lopsided blonde pigtails and skinned knees. I'd chopped off my hair and dyed it, so

I had a white-blonde pixie thing going on. It was perfect for spending long hours in a hot kitchen, and it was easy to maintain. But I didn't look all that different. "Since he doesn't have one, I'm not surprised."

He laughed and flashed a charming smile that was concealed by a thick, brown beard that gave him a rakish air. "Okay, then, whoever you are. I'm Savior."

I smiled politely. "Nice to meet you." *Again.* "So, that drink?"

"I'll meet you there. I know the place well."

I smiled and slid into the rental, wondering what his reaction would be when he finally realized who I was. His best friend's kid sister.

***

"Shit. Fuck. Shit, shit, fuck … goddammit!"

I woke up to the sound of a deep, angry and totally male voice, grunting curse words into the early morning air. It took a moment to fully wake up and realize who and what was happening, but when I did, I groaned. "Keep it down."

"You should have fucking told me," the angry male said.

Wide awake now, I sat up with no thoughts about modesty even as his blue eyes tracked down to my chest. "Told you what, exactly?"

His look turned dark and not in the sexy way he'd devoured me last night before we got naked and then got lost in our collective grief. "That you're Ammo's fucking sister!"

Now angry, I stood and fisted my hands on my hips. "How in the hell would I know you didn't recognize me? Do you make a habit of fucking people you barely know?" I held up a hand because I really did *not* want to know the answer to that. "I don't care. It's done, and we can't change it, but if you have that much of a problem with it, you should leave."

He spluttered, outraged and obviously feeling guilty. It was displayed all over his handsome, angry face. Too bad for him I didn't give a flying fuck about his guilt.

"You're Ammo's kid sister."

"Yeah and he's dead so it doesn't matter!" That reminder had tears pricking behind my eyes, but I refused to let them fall. I couldn't. If I started crying now, I was worried that I wouldn't be able to stop and that was something I couldn't afford to do. I had to be strong. Well, *stronger*. I was on my own now. There was no soft place to land, no parachute to guide me down and no fallback plan. So, I pushed down those tears and stared him down. "I want you to leave."

He stared for so long I thought he might refuse, but I should have known better. Savior had 'love 'em and leave 'em' written all over his face. "I'm sorry, Mandy. I shouldn't have let that happen. It was a mistake."

"Got it," I told him and wrapped my arms around my waist. I wouldn't let him see how his words gutted me. Nothing like the sting of cold hard rejection to soothe the ache of loss, right? "Then leaving, right now, shouldn't be a problem."

He nodded and stepped into his jeans, because apparently that was appropriate funeral attire for the Reckless Bastards. "Do you need anything?"

"Only for you to leave."

"But -"

I shook my head. "Just leave." There was nothing else to say and even if there was, I had no interest in talking to him. I had one day to get what was left in my childhood home packed up and ready for the realtor to put it on the market, before heading back to New York to finish up my pastry apprenticeship. I had six weeks to go, and then I would return to Vegas and start working at *Knead*, the best damn place for pastries in the whole state.

And pretend the last twenty-four hours never happened.

KB WINTERS

Chapter 1

Mandy

It's been months since I made the move back to Las Vegas, but it still felt surreal being here. No matter where I went, the supermarket, the hairdresser, the park, I expected to see Ammo's loose-legged walk and dimpled smile coming my way, a smart retort on the tip of his tongue. But working at *Knead* kept me busy, which I needed in order to keep me from succumbing to the darkness that always seemed to hover around the edges of my life. Right now, my life was boring and completely predictable and I knew that sounded terrible, but to me it was perfect.

I'd plenty of excitement in my life. Losing both of my parents tragically and then my brother, living on the streets of Las Vegas while said brother was off fighting a war that hadn't yet taken him from me. So, boring suited me just fine. I didn't go out on my days off from work, just relaxed at home catching up on chores, my favorite television shows and reading trashy romance. Some days it felt as though I would die of boredom but it would be preferable to dying any other way.

But even the work day had to end, and at a little after seven I removed my apron and chef hat, grabbed my bag, and exited through the back of the restaurant. The parking lot wasn't all that well lit, but I had pepper spray on my keychain and my biggest key clutched between my fingers, a trick all girls from the big city learn early. Or else.

"Yo, Mandy!"

I froze at the sound of my name. Other than the people at *Knead*, I didn't know anyone in this city any longer, which meant it was someone I *used* to know. I turned slowly, ready to pounce if I needed to. Instead I only had to bite back a groan at the sight of my former friend, and I mean that in the loosest definition of the word.

"Krissy."

DELICIOUSLY DAMAGED

She hadn't changed much in the last decade, a little older with a few gray sprouts, more noticeable because of her shiny black hair. She had a few fine lines around her pale blue eyes and she was thinner than she used to be, but otherwise she looked exactly the same.

"I heard you were back."

"I am."

I left this place ten years ago and she was a big part of the reason why. I did plenty of shit I wasn't proud of back then, all in the name of survival, and I didn't regret it. For me though, it couldn't go on forever. Using a fake I.D. in a city like this was asking for trouble. And card counting? Plenty of people had ended up buried in the desert for that particular sin. I had a knack for counting cards even as a teenager, and Krissy was quick to pick up on it and capitalize on it. She finagled a way to get me the I.D. so we could take the casinos for enough cash to make it from one month to the next.

"How've you been?" She looked at me now, the same way she did when I was sixteen and alone for the first time in my life. Like a predator who found the biggest, juiciest target just lying around.

"I'm good, Krissy. You?"

"Better now that you're back. I missed you."

I snorted my disbelief at that. "Right. What's this about?"

"You don't believe me?"

"No, I don't. We were useful to each other, but that's it. *If you leave, you're dead to me.* Remember?" She'd said those words to me the night before I put this fucking town in my rear view. Krissy wanted to scam and scheme forever. Not me. I wanted more out of life.

She brushed the words away with a dismissive flip of her hand. "I was upset." She smiled in the way she used to do that I'd always mistook for care. It was plain old manipulation. "How long have you been back?"

"A while."

"You weren't going to look me up?"

"No."

DELICIOUSLY DAMAGED

I'd hopped on a bus that took me all the way to the other side of the country but I'd only gotten as far as Colorado before I realized Krissy wasn't my friend. And had never been my friend.

"Then I guess it's a good thing I found you because —"

I held up a hand. "You can stop right there. I didn't come back for you or for that and I'm not doing it, so whatever you're thinking you better find someone else." I walked away, still staring at Krissy because I didn't trust her as far as I could throw her scrawny ass.

"It's like that now?"

I nodded and her friendly smile hardened. "I need your help."

"I can't help you."

"You can," she insisted.

"Fine, then I won't." She glared at me and walked away. I had a feeling, though, it wouldn't be the last I saw of the woman who taught me that no one could be trusted.

By the time I made it back to the shithole apartment I rented, I was in a bad mood and ready to fight someone. Anyone. I hated seeing Krissy again, reminding me of who I used to be. More importantly, of how stupid and naïve I used to be. Never again.

"Ugh!" I said out loud to the closet as I kicked off my shoes. I hated that seeing her brought up all those memories and emotions. Feelings I'd worked hard to bury ever since a certain blue-eyed biker reminded me why feelings were total bullshit.

I made a sub and killed three beers while I binge-watched TV until I passed out on the sofa. I'd nearly made it a full night without thinking about Ammo.

***

My first day off in almost two weeks and I'd decided to spend it tracking Savior down. I must be out of my mind to willingly face the source of my greatest rejection. But I knew returning my brother's leather vest with the Reckless Bastards insignia to his other family would mean a lot to Ammo. Which meant it was, literally, the least I could do.

After I spent the morning cleaning my apartment, doing a load of laundry and picking up groceries, I jumped in my used blue sedan and made my way to the converted airplane hangar that was their clubhouse. The closer I came to the frosted glass doors, the more anxious I became and with a striking blonde standing sentry at the door, overnight shipping seemed like a better option. Then she turned her head toward the sun and a serene smile tilted her full lips. "Now that's a smile I'd kill to have," I told her honestly, startling her.

"You can have the smile, it was as phony as a two-dollar bill."

Funny. I introduced myself because I wasn't a caveman and because I wanted to assure her I wasn't here to snag one of her biker boyfriends. "Mandy."

"Teddy," she said. "I'm Teddy and I'm only here because my babysitter made me come." Her smile was genuine this time, filled with a hint of sarcasm and mischief.

I couldn't remember the last time I'd had a real conversation like this with another woman, or with anyone really. Despite the sexist views of society that women belonged in the kitchen, professional kitchens were dominated by men. Even on the pastry side, dicks ruled the world. But Teddy was edgy and kind of snarky, a contrast to her classic beauty. "I'm just here to return something to … the club." No need to mention Savior.

Her eyes flashed with recognition and we spent a few minutes discussing the write-up I'd gotten and asking me about wedding cakes. She wanted something special for a friend, wanted to know if I was up for it.

I nodded and she said, "My bag is inside, but please don't leave without exchanging contact info."

I promised, feeling awkward as a tall, gorgeous man with long blond hair exited and took a protective stance behind her. "Nice to meet you," I told her and steeled my nerves to go inside when Savior came out. "Just the person I came to see."

"Mandy? What are you doing here?" He looked at me warily, like I was planning to make a scene. Typical man. Give him one night of hot sex and he thinks you're ready to wear his ring.

"Don't worry," I told him as he led me to escape a loud gang of partiers. We found our way down a dark hall to a stark room with a twin bed, a dresser and photos of bikini-clad women on the wall. "I'm not here for a repeat performance. This was in some of the things I put in storage after the funeral. I know Ammo would want you guys to have it." I handed him the jacket, making sure our fingers didn't touch at all. That was a temptation I didn't need or want.

"You should have told me," he said, just as my hand landed on the doorknob. His voice was deep and angry, eager like he'd been waiting for a chance to get this off his chest.

I sighed and whirled on him, now pissed off. Between Savior's indignation, Krissy's harassment and my boss Landry's total asshole-ness, I was losing my grasp on patience.

"You've known me since I was a little girl, Savior. How in the hell was I supposed to know you didn't recognize me? You never *asked* for my name so I assumed it was because you *knew* it."

In hindsight, I should have realized that between the Reckless Bitches, his biker swagger and handsome face that he probably fucked plenty of nameless women. "Anyway, that's why I came here, to give you Ammo's jacket. Nothing more."

"*Kutte,*" he said, correcting me on the leather jacket.

"Whatever. Have a nice life." I yanked the door open and hooked a left until I heard the noise of the group we passed on our way to the room with more privacy.

"Mandy, wait!"

I froze and turned, waiting for him to say more. "If you, ah, need anything —"

DELICIOUSLY DAMAGED

"I don't. I'm fine on my own." I didn't need or want the Reckless Bastards' help in general, or his help specifically.

"Ammo would want —"

I cut him off. "Ammo is dead, Savior. Whatever loyalty you had to him, doesn't extend to me. Goodbye."

I soaked in his rugged handsomeness for several long seconds before forcing my gaze and my feet to move away from the tall, imposing figure he cut. Savior was nice to look at and even better in bed but he'd made his feelings about fucking me very clear. The further I got away from him and the clubhouse, the more my heart rate would settle and the calmer I'd feel.

Knowing what was waiting for me at my shoebox apartment, nothing but mindless entertainment, I decided to take a trip to the cemetery. Visit the only people in the world who had ever truly cared about me. At least they were all together now, and as I sat on the prickly grass in front of the three headstones, I knew they were the reason I'd come back to Vegas. I thought there was nothing for me here, but it turns out everything that mattered to me was right here.

Which meant I wasn't going anywhere. Not anytime soon, anyway.

Chapter 2

Savior

"Herman Redding's farm was raided and *not* by the fucking Feds. He's our biggest supplier." Everything about Cross screamed stress and pissed the fuck off. Redding was the biggest supplier for the club's dispensaries, but thankfully not the only one or we'd be shit out of luck when the supply ran out. "His crops were burned in the middle of the night. The government might be assholes but they wouldn't do that."

He was right about that. I looked around the Church table, with one empty seat for our missing brother Gunnar, at the other members of the club who wore looks that ranged from pissed and ready to fight, to worried we might be in for some major conflict. Not that the Reckless Bastards ever backed down from a fucking fight, but with grass and ass legal, there was no reason to ever get caught up with the fucking law. "It had to be done by another MC. The burns were too clean and efficient, definitely not some shit a tweaker could do."

Cross nodded. He was confident in my assessment because fire, bombs, guns – it was all in my wheelhouse. I was an explosives expert in the military, Sergeant at Arms for the club and I liked to fuck shit up. "The lines were clean to make sure not one crop remained so I'm inclined to agree. We need to find out who, though."

His gaze scanned each member sitting around the table, letting them know this was serious shit. "We need to up security at our dispensaries, which means security defaults to the brothers who can legally carry. Those of you who can't, go talk to our other suppliers and see if they need security help. We take in too much cash to lose this income."

"Roadkill MC just opened a dispensary, so we should start with them," I offered, knowing those fuckers had no fucking limits.

Jag pounded his fist on the table and kicked his chair back to stand up. "I'll dig into their digital shit, see what pops up."

Jag, despite his quiet demeanor, was a badass motherfucker. He could kill a man at a thousand yards or dismantle his life with nothing more than an internet connection.

"Good," Cross said and pounded on the table. "Church over." Most of the brothers made a quick exit but Cross eyed me in that way that said he wanted to talk. Dammit.

"What's up?"

"Was that Mandy I saw in here the other day?"

I blinked. How in the hell had he recognized her? "Yeah it was." I knew he expected me to say more but what the fuck else was there to say?

He glared. "Ammo might be dead but he's still our brother, which makes her family. We are all she has, Savior. Don't fuck with her if you don't mean it."

I laughed. "Yeah, well I already told her that and she told me with Ammo gone we could fucking forget about her. Besides," I grinned, trying to lighten the mood as I patted my chest. "I always mean it at the time." Which was a dick thing to say, especially given the way shit went down with Mandy.

If the dark scowl he wore was anything to go by, Cross wasn't amused. He raked a hand through unruly brown hair and blew out a breath. "Just don't fuck her, okay?" My face must have given something away because he groaned and smacked the table. Hard. "Seriously? How long has she even been in town?"

"It was at the funeral. I didn't know she was Mandy when it happened. I didn't handle it well, which probably has something to do with why she wants fuck all to do with me. Or the club."

Not that I blamed her. I was a prick and she should steer clear of me. Mandy was a girl meant for picket fences and two point five kids, all that regular shit. I wasn't that guy and never would be.

DELICIOUSLY DAMAGED

Cross's eyes darkened damn near to black. "That's too bad, Savior. She is under our protection whether she wants it or not. Whether she asks for it or not. Always."

He was right. That's how we rolled. Except for expelled brothers, Reckless Bastards protected their own. I nodded at my Prez to let him know I heard him loud and clear. "I'll make it right." Or I would try. Mandy was different now, hard with sharp edges. Distant. Except for those few hours in bed, she didn't reveal much emotion or any other clues to her feelings. Even angry, she was as blank as stone.

"See that you do," he said and left Church.

I followed him a few minutes later, making sure the door was locked tight. Church was our sacred club space where we discussed business on all sides of the law. The room couldn't be hacked, bugged or breached in anyway. Even the door was reinforced because we protected our shit.

I needed to clear my head though, so I took long strides through the clubhouse, ignoring two of the

Reckless Bitches eager to get my attention. The best way to clear my head was to fuck some shit up, so I crossed the parking lot and headed for the gun range where I found Max grumbling about wedding shit. He and Jana, his ball and chain, had a double header coming up. They had a bun in the oven and were getting hitched soon. "Hey man, quit your bitching. I need the biggest gun we have to shoot some shit up!"

Max looked up with a wide grin. "Fuck yeah!" He got down a few of the ones we kept for times just like this. Max and I laughed like kids, whooping it up as we wrecked the paper targets and turned our attention to the outdoor targets fixed on hay bales. "Good idea, man. This wedding shit is stressing me out."

"Yeah, life is stressing me out," I grunted and squeezed the trigger before he could ask any damn questions about it. So we shot and then shot some more, going through a few boxes of ammo before we tired ourselves out.

When we were done Max found his opening. "Want to talk about it?"

DELICIOUSLY DAMAGED

I looked at him like he'd lost his mind. "Fuck no! Hell, I don't know. I don't wanna talk about this shit."

He barked out a loud laugh. "Spoken like a man with no woman to pull his feelings out of him, whether he wants to talk about it or not."

Shaking his head, Max looked like a man who loved every minute of talking about his feelings with his curvy little bride to be. "So, who's the girl?"

I let out a loud grunt as I took apart the rifle and cleaned it. "Doesn't matter. I was an asshole after we had sex and she's pissed. Wants nothing at all to do with me."

The bastard clapped me on the back. "You mean that famous Savior charm can't make her forget?"

"Shit, she might try to filet my nuts if I even try," I sighed and put the gun away. "But she's Ammo's sister so I have to at least apologize or deal with fucking Cross."

Max hadn't known Ammo all that well, because he'd been recalled to the Army and wasn't around all that much.

"Shit, bro. That's rough."

"Tell me about it." I rolled my eyes. "Anyway, I need to clear my head so I'll stick around here. Go convince your woman to take care of all the wedding shit."

"All right. Thanks you crazy bastard," he said, waving as he walked away.

"Hey asshole, that's Reckless Bastard to you!" I laughed, feeling a little better than I did before I unleashed hundreds of bullets on that paper target.

Progress.

***

I gave Mandy the weekend to calm down before I decided to approach her and offer up an apology she might actually listen to. Hopefully. My first stop was the restaurant where she worked. *Knead* was an elegant, great-looking place that specialized in pastries and other sweet treats. The perky hostess told me she'd already left for the day. I had no idea where she lived since she'd already sold the house she and Ammo had lived in for most of their lives.

I crossed the parking lot back to my bike when I spotted Mandy and two rough looking dudes walking after her a little faster than I liked. I turned and started in her direction, picking up speed when one of the guys started talking to her.

"We're trying to be nice about this, Mandy. What a sweet name that is," he said, licking his lips and reaching for her, laughing when she smacked his hand away.

"You'll never know."

I smiled, proud of how she handled herself even though I couldn't hear most of what was being said. I could see it, though and the conversation was heated. Tense.

Both guys moved in closer, trying to intimidate Mandy and failing. She was tough, but guys like that got off on fear and they would do anything to make sure she was afraid. One of them, the shorter one, pulled back his hand to strike her. "Just agree to this one little job and we'll leave you alone."

I had the element of surprise as I grabbed the asshole's wrist. "I wouldn't do that if I were you." My voice was a low, menacing growl as the asshole turned and grinned.

"This has nothing to do with you, fucker. Step away."

Even Mandy glared at me. "It doesn't," she confirmed coldly but I didn't move. And I wouldn't until they were gone, and she was safe.

The taller one took a step closer and leaned forward until he and Mandy were eye to eye. "Next time we see you, we won't be so nice about it. And we won't be asking."

DELICIOUSLY DAMAGED

I had no clue what the fuck they were talking about and I knew Mandy wouldn't let on, so I waited. Ready to have her back because I knew she'd never ask for help. Hitching her bag higher on her shoulder, I noticed she had a large key poking between her middle and forefingers.

"And next time I see you, I'll shoot first and ask questions later. So run along boys."

She made a *shooing* motion, watching them until they were far enough away she could turn without danger.

I was right behind her, ready to talk. "I don't suppose you want to tell me what that was about?"

"Nope, I don't. And I don't need your help. I'm perfectly capable of taking care of myself."

"No one said otherwise," I told her, working hard to tamp down my frustration at how pigheaded she was being. "When the hell did you become so stubborn?"

She pulled open the door and tossed her bag over to the passenger seat before turning to me. "What is it that you wanted, Savior?"

"I was hoping we could talk. Actually, I want to talk to you, Mandy. I owe you an apology."

"No you don't, and I don't want one. See you around, dude," she said in a tone that indicated she hoped she wouldn't ever see me again. Even still, I jogged back to my bike and followed her home from a safe distance, just to make sure she didn't have any other visitors or unwelcome guests. At least that was what I told myself. I refused to believe it had to do with the memories of our night together that I couldn't shake.

Not that my reasons mattered when Mandy couldn't even stand to be around me for more than a few minutes. I couldn't go there. Hell, I wouldn't. Not again.

But what I could do, was keep an eye out for her. Keep her safe because we all owed Ammo—and her—that much.

Chapter 3

Mandy

"Those egg whites are *not* stiff enough!" Landry, the executive pastry chef at *Knead,* barked at me without regard to how his love of raw onions offended my senses. And my eyes. "And don't think for one second I'll take it easy on you because you're a girl," he sniveled. He was such a fucking weasel, never mind a misogynist, and if given the chance to do so without going to prison, I'd punch him in the throat. With a mallet.

"First of all, I am a woman *chef*—not a girl. And I've never asked you to take it easy on me." I flipped the bowl over, confident in my skills. "If these egg whites get any stiffer we'll use them to stack bricks outside." They were perfect and that wasn't ego, it was experience. I'd done it enough times to know the difference.

"Yeah, well, you make sure you keep it that way." Whatever the fuck *that* meant. He walked away, griping under his breath loud enough for the whole kitchen to hear.

I hated his guts, more than even my most difficult instructor in culinary school. The man's ego was based on two years of rave reviews plus a few prestigious awards, which he'd earned. Twenty years ago. He refused to change with the times, instead hiring talented chefs and taking credit for their work. Until they realized what a prick he was and quit. I had a feeling I would be just another pastry chef who "used to work for Landry." If I didn't kill him first.

We'd gotten along fine at first. Then the write up in Vegas Magazine happened and well, his ego still hadn't recovered. It wasn't my problem and I refused to let him get a rise out of me. As long as he knew I expected to be treated with respect, he could be a blowhard. I was used to it.

"We do not allow visitors at work, Mandy!" he barked across the entire kitchen, startling everyone as their eyes turned to me.

"Is this restaurant not inside of a hotel and casino?"

Because members of the press often showed up to speak with the chefs and Landry had no problem as long as they pretended to admire him.

"You have a visitor," he sniffed, glaring at me like that was supposed to frighten me. "Did you tell them that you *don't allow visitors*?"

I knew I was pushing it, but honestly, I was beyond caring. Moving back to this god-forsaken place had proven to be a huge mistake for a few reasons. At his glare, I shrugged.

"Guess not."

I took a few minutes to get the piping perfect on the custard that would be part of the *prix fixe* menu before wiping my hands and leaving the kitchen. Since I had no friends or family to speak of, I could only imagine who the visitor could be. I wasn't at all surprised to find Krissy leaning against the skinny wooden podium, popping her gum.

"What do you want?"

She flashed a fake grin and sauntered outside, leaving me to follow.

"Is that how you greet an old friend?"

"Friends? Is that what we were?" My memory recalled it differently but now wasn't the time.

"I'd like to think so." She shrugged as she lit a Newport 100, her favorite brand of cigarettes. "But maybe now that you've got a big fancy life, you forgot."

"I didn't forget anything. I remember all of it, but that doesn't mean I'm going back. I'm not."

"Just one job, Mandy. This one tournament. Blackjack. It's a quarter of a mil to the winner. Imagine what we could do with that kind of money!" She practically salivated at the thought of the cash that she would, no doubt, spend in just a few months. "Can't you just do this for me?"

DELICIOUSLY DAMAGED

That yanked a bitter laugh from somewhere deep inside me. "No. I did that to survive, Krissy. I'm not taking that kind of risk again."

Her blue eyes narrowed and I knew things were about to get ugly. Krissy was, at heart, a used car salesman. When false flattery and fake promises didn't work, she turned cutthroat. "I don't remember you being such a bitch."

"Yeah, well, I was a vulnerable kid back then, and I bought what you were selling a lot easier when I didn't know any better." She could try to deny all she wanted, but I knew the truth.

She narrowed her eyes at me. "When you needed me, I was there for you."

I laughed again, but this time it wasn't bitter and it definitely wasn't amused. It was anger. Rage. "There for me? I asked you to help me get a fake I.D. and somehow you ended up taking a cut of all the winnings when I took all the risk. Sorry, but I'm not so stupid anymore."

Arms crossed, she placed the filter between thin, heavily wrinkled lips from too much sun and too much cigarette smoke, pulling hard until that hit of nicotine soothed her frayed edges. "I could make life very difficult for you in this city, Mandy."

"And I can make it just as difficult for you, Krissy. Why do you need the money so bad? You owe someone you can't pay?"

That quick flash of fear told me I was right. "If you or your friends think you can threaten me, you all better think again. I don't scare so easily, so think long and hard about your next move."

She stomped her foot like a five-year-old. "But this tourney is easy money. You'll definitely place. Third place is fifty grand."

"No." It was that simple. I had plenty of reasons that I didn't want to do it, but none of them mattered. I wouldn't step foot inside a casino to count cards unless the only other option was starvation, and that would never happen because any greasy spoon or chain restaurant in this city would be happy to have me.

"If you don't do this, there will be trouble. It's not a threat," she said, suddenly sounding terrified. "It's a guarantee."

I took a step closer and glared at her. "Then you should have thought about that shit before you shot off your mouth to those thugs. Whatever you think you can do to make me do this, just know that I can do worse. And I will."

She looked worried, but I knew this wasn't over. Krissy owed someone a lot of money and my guess was those thugs who accosted me the other day in the parking lot were part of that *someone's* organization.

They would be back, of that much I was certain.

What they didn't know was that I would be ready.

KB WINTERS

Chapter 4

Savior

"What are you doing here, man?"

Lasso's smile was wide and friendly when I stepped into GET INK'D, his arms draped over two hot sorority girls.

"Too many Bitches at the clubhouse, a man can't even get a fucking drink in peace."

There were nearly a dozen lounging around in their tightest, lowest cut outfits to attract attention. The Reckless Bitches served their purpose but sometimes a man just needed to *be*.

"What's up around here?"

His smile spread even wider if that was possible. "I'm going to give Katie and Becca tattoos. On their hipbones." He emphasized the words, flashing me his best horndog grin over their heads. The man had as much charm as the state he came from, and the chicks ate that shit up. The sorority girls looked up at him like he couldn't possibly be real. Too bad they'd be disappointed that he was only there for a few nights.

"You here for ink?"

"Nope, just here." I was bored, restless and in search of something to do. Lasso disappeared with the sorority girls and I found Jag bent over a big ass biker who had 'weekend warrior' written all over him. He was big and bald, and had no visible tats, like someone who had a nine to five to go to every week. They were easy to spot, but they were good people, and most importantly, they kept guys like us, the real deal, flush with business. They came to us for tats, grass, ass and guns.

"Hey Jag."

"Sup, Savior," he said without looking up. His concentration had always been one of his most admirable traits. "Golden Boy is in with a customer, but she's decent."

DELICIOUSLY DAMAGED

I nodded at the biker doing his best to look cool as I walked by. "Thanks man." I hoped Golden Boy was able to get away for a few hours, maybe go for a ride to clear the fucking cobwebs from my head. I knocked and waited, feeling agitated and impatient.

"Come in," his gruff voice called, but it was less gruff now that he'd gone and fallen in love with a former model with a sharp tongue and long legs.

I pushed the door open and the smile on my face died when I spotted Mandy sitting in his chair.

"What the hell are you doing here?"

I ignored the sharp look Golden Boy sent me, waiting for Mandy to answer.

She stared up at me, her expression blank and emotionless.

"I would think that's obvious." She turned back to him, dismissing me. "Privacy would be nice," she said tersely.

Golden Boy flashed an apologetic grin at me and pushed the door closed in my face.

"Dammit!" I smacked the door, letting my anger get the better of me. Why the fuck was I so angry, anyway? Mandy was just my friend's little sister and a chick I fucked. Once. I couldn't let her get to me like this. Shit, I refused to. But I knew what was bothering me. Her anger and refusal to talk to me, combined with Cross's words. *She's like family. Under our protection.* Both of those things were true no matter how either of us felt about it, which made this the perfect chance to make her listen to my apology.

Twenty minutes later, Golden Boy and Mandy exited the room, all smiles and laughter.

"I'm not sure if I'll be able to make it, Tate. But you can let Teddy know I did get the details. And not to worry that she didn't hire me to do the cake. No way I could have transported a five-tier beauty down to San Diego."

"Yeah, well she felt bad after promising you the gig," Tate said, flashing a warm smile that spoke of familiarity.

DELICIOUSLY DAMAGED

"Listen, we're good. She's gonna love the pastry chef I recommended."

She rolled her eyes affectionately, like they had some kind of friendship I didn't know about.

"As long as you show up," he warned,

"I'll do what I can, but my boss hates me so I can't guarantee he'll give me the time off. I need a tube of that ointment," she pointed to the aftercare ointment on the shelf behind him, paid and waved him off like they were old friends. "Catch you later, Tate." She walked right past me, exiting the shop without a glance, or even the fucking evil eye, aimed at me.

I stood, feeling wound up. Anxious. Hell, I didn't know, but I knew the source and I followed her out of the shop and caught up with her halfway up the block.

"You're avoiding me."

She didn't answer and I took another step closer.

"And now you're ignoring me."

She sighed, frustrated and barely hanging on to her rage.

"You are not a part of my life, Savior. I don't need to avoid or ignore you because we're nothing to each other. Two people who once fucked, that's it. There's no reason to pretend it was anything else, which means I don't need you checking up on me."

"I've known you since you were a little girl, Mandy. That's more than two people who once fucked," I told her, throwing her words back at her.

"No. You *knew* me, back when I was a kid. A lot of time and a lot of life has happened since then. You don't know shit about me or my life."

The way she said it told me there was shit in her life. I asked myself, should I have known about it? I'd promised Ammo that me and the club would look after her when we could. My last tour with Ammo was my last tour before I left the Army, but I'd come home and gotten caught up in the club. "So, tell me."

DELICIOUSLY DAMAGED

She laughed and it was filled with bitterness and anger. "I don't think so."

I leaned on her car, staring across the hood. "So, this is how it's gonna be? You pretending we don't know each other."

She shrugged. "It won't be hard because we *don't* know each other. Just forget we used to know each other, all right?"

"I can't."

"Try harder." She yanked her door open and jumped inside, rolling her eyes.

I stepped back when she started the engine, feeling even more frustrated than ever, and curious as hell about what had happened to her in the years since we'd known each other.

Guilt was weighing me down as she disappeared from my view, so I hopped on my bike and rode until my hands tensed with pain. I still didn't feel any fucking better.

"You want to do *what*?" I couldn't believe my ears. Max Ellison had called Church to discuss his fucking destination wedding. In California.

"You heard me. Jana wants to get married at some fancy ass hotel in San Diego, so that's what we're doing. All of us. You got a problem with that?" His frown was fierce but I didn't back down from a fight. Not even from one of my brothers.

I was the first one to speak up. "You want to go out of town for a full goddamn week when someone is targeting our business?" I was all for a man finding a woman he wanted to fuck forever but business was business. And right now, someone was fucking with businesses that belonged to the Reckless Bastards.

"The old timers and the prospects will be here. But if that's your biggest concern, stay here Savior." The way he said it, like a threat, made my hackles rise but I kept my mouth shut because he was right. We were friends *and* brothers, and I wasn't going to miss his wedding.

"Fine, I'll be there to watch you get hitched to the old ball and chain. Just make sure we're covered."

"We're covered," Cross assured me and I knew he'd tell me more later.

"The Bitches aren't invited," Max said, narrowing his gaze around the table to make sure everyone understood. They hadn't made Jana feel very welcome and I didn't blame her for keeping them away from her special day.

Cross nodded again.

Lasso smacked the table. "Woo-eee! San Diego has plenty of sweet ass to go around." He grinned. "I'll even bring a Stetson or two. Ladies love a cowboy."

Jag laughed and punched his arm. "They love those tight ass pants you wear, that's all."

"Try it sometime, you might get some action from someone other than your hand." Lasso laughed, cracking himself up.

"All right, any new business?" Cross looked around the room, his expression serious as fuck. "No? Then we're done."

Thank fuck. I was on my feet and walking away when Max caught up to me. "What's your beef with Mandy?"

"I have no beef with her, or anyone," I said a little too innocently based on his skeptical expression.

"Cut the shit. Tate said you acted like a real asshole to her at his shop. He also said she gave you the cold shoulder."

True. "Why is she even invited to your wedding?"

"Not that I owe you an explanation, but Teddy likes her and so does Jana. They're trying to become her friends so whatever your problem with her is, get over it. Or keep your distance."

"Fine," I told him with a little more anger than I really felt and a whole lot more than he deserved. Then I walked away. Max was right. I had no excuse for my behavior. Hell, even I didn't know what was wrong with me.

Maybe I should just keep my distance.

KB WINTERS

Chapter 5

Mandy

Another shift over and I felt pretty damn good. A few different tables had requested my presence to rave about my profiteroles with Irish cream and brandy infused chocolate. Landry hated it, called it elementary and derivative, which I admitted, it might be. But it was also a customer favorite and usually sold out before lunch was over. A well-known morning show duet who filmed live daily in Las Vegas raved about them on air last week and Landry had reluctantly agreed to let me make more. His sour mood couldn't dampen mine, though, because it was nice to know someone out there appreciated the way I sweated my ass off in the Führer's kitchen.

My smile dimmed as I pushed back into the kitchen, breezing by Landry's extra round midsection and heavy breathing like I didn't notice it.

"I hope you told them that your supposed genius was *all* under my instruction," he barked.

I said nothing in reply as I removed my apron, hat and chef's coat, grabbed my shit and got the fuck out of Dodge. If I stayed another minute I might say — or do — something that would get me fired. Nothing could dampen my mood, not today. I pushed the door open and felt the hot desert sun beat down on my face.

"That's the shit," I practically purred. You'd think I wouldn't want to feel the sun after spending ten hours in a hot kitchen with nearly a dozen ovens going at once. But the fresh air and sunshine was just what I needed.

Apparently, Krissy hadn't gotten the message to stay away.

"Get off my car," I told her, my tone dark and threatening.

Eyes wide, she pushed off, and crossed her arms. Doing her best to look tough.

"Or what?"

DELICIOUSLY DAMAGED

"Krissy, don't fuck with me today." She didn't move quick enough and I invaded her space, close enough that I could smell the cigarette stink with every breath.

"I'll leave you alone, when you agree."

I laughed. Between her and Savior, I was all full up on people from my past coming back to haunt me. It made me reconsider the intelligence of moving back to this damn city.

"I'll never agree, Krissy. No matter what you and your thugs think you can do to scare me. I'll just push back even harder."

Her thin lips curled into a sneer. "It would be a shame if your new employer found out about your past, somehow."

And now we've moved on to other threats. "Go right ahead and maybe I'll talk to the casinos about your ruthless scams." Her eyes grew wide because she knew they would ban her sorry ass before the sun set on the day.

"You wouldn't."

"Try me." I stepped even closer so she had to lean back to gain some distance. "I'm not some scared, lonely teenager anymore, Krissy. Whatever you *think* you can do to me, just remember it goes both ways."

I pointed a finger at the center of her head. "If you can't take a hint," I applied just enough pressure to let this bitch know I meant business before pulling back. "I'll be happy to make it easier to understand. Got it?"

She nodded, her eyes filled with fear and uncertainty. I knew what it was about. Krissy was used to me like I used to be, scared, lonely and desperate for a connection. But she'd been the one to cure me of those useless emotions. In New York, I hardened my heart against the world, but it hadn't been fully turned to stone until I got the visit at school from a man and a woman in Army dress uniforms telling me my last family member had been killed in action.

Action. They said it like it was a fucking football game or a white water rafting adventure, not fucking war. So yeah, I wasn't afraid. Of anything. Not anymore.

"Just because I got it," Krissy called as I backed away from her, "doesn't mean *they* will."

"You can all give it your best shot," I told her, not taking my eyes off her until her back was to me. I was pretty sure the guys from the parking lot were part of some type of gang, but no one bullied me. Not anymore.

"Mandy!"

I turned and gave her a cool stare, waiting for her next words.

"If you don't do this, I'm in deep shit."

"Then maybe you should have tried to talk to me instead of threatening me or sending your goons after me. Because honestly, I don't give a shit about you or your problems."

I didn't miss the tears shining in her eyes; they did nothing for me. I didn't soften at the sight of tears, which were probably for show anyway. Her emotions, hell, most people's emotions didn't impact me at all these days, and that was just how I liked it.

***

After burying Ammo something in me had died and I knew it — felt it — but I didn't want to do anything about it. I'd isolated myself from everyone, and after the funeral and Savior, my transformation was complete. For a few brief minutes in the afterglow of spectacular sex, I felt a tiny bubble of relief. But his reaction had not only ruined the moment, his regret reminded me why I'd spent the past few years keeping my distance from the world. Aside from too brief and too infrequent talks to Ammo and obligatory outings with my classmates and professors in culinary school, I kept to myself.

It was better that way. And I reminded myself of that fact as I took the short drive back to my apartment, staring at the bleak, square building where I lived. There was nothing wrong with it, aside from being old and ugly. It was affordable and that was what mattered. I was all about pinching pennies these days. The money from the sale of the house plus Ammo's life insurance and death gratuity from the military was adding to my nice little nest egg that I would use to open my own restaurant one day. Or, based on the past few weeks, start a new life somewhere else.

Savior was waiting for me after I emptied out my car and reached my apartment, leaning against the railing expectantly, but I walked right past him like I didn't see him. I was in no mood for another confrontation. Not today. I entered my apartment and locked the door behind me, scanning the small room to see if anything had been disturbed. The truth was, Krissy and her friends had me a little paranoid. And after the shit that had gone down with Teddy a few weeks ago, I wasn't taking my safety for granted. Luckily nothing had been disturbed this time, so I relaxed.

Until a loud knock startled me out of my thoughts. I knew who it was and debated, for a least a moment, ignoring the knock. But Savior was a stubborn fucker and he wouldn't go away, so I pulled the door open just enough to look at his handsome, arrogant face.

"What?"

He took a step forward but my grip tightened on the doorknob and I planted my foot firmly behind the door. If he wanted to, he could get in, but he'd have to use some force because I wouldn't let him in. Not again.

"Let me in, Mandy."

"No. Tell me what you want or go away. Those are your options."

We stared at each other for several long, tense moments before he let out a long, frustrated breath.

"I just want to clear the air."

Of course he did. For some reason he was determined to hang onto some misguided sense of loyalty to my brother where I was concerned.

"I don't need any air cleared, Savior. You don't owe me a damn thing."

"I disagree. Your brother—"

DELICIOUSLY DAMAGED

"—is dead. He's never coming back and you coming around here won't change that fact. He was dead when you fucked me and regretted it, so again, don't worry about me."

He stared at me like he didn't recognize me, and why should he? He'd never known me as anything more than an energetic little girl completely enamored with her big brother.

"I'm sorry," he grunted out. "And if we could just talk —"

"Apparently you have a hearing problem," I told him, my voice hard and cold before I slammed the door in his face and locked it, letting out a long, shuddery breath. I needed time to myself, to decompress after what had started off as a pretty decent day. Until it was just about over.

I washed off the day and whipped up a quick veggie sub for dinner, curled up on the sofa and watched TV until I fell asleep and the TV watched me.

I woke up the next day, ready to do it all over again.

***

I stepped from the hot shower, cursing my lack of foresight for not choosing an apartment with a big, deep tub that I could soak in after spending all day bent over a waist-high table. But comfort wasn't really my aim when I signed the lease on this place, just its proximity to work and the dirt-cheap rent. It was just above a crack hotel in terms of price, cleanliness and safety, but a deadbolt from the hardware store took care of the last one and that was all I cared about. A shower wasn't a hot soak, but my muscles felt looser and I no longer had the urge to kill anyone. In my book, that was a win.

I had just slipped into a thick pair of wool socks over my workout pants that hadn't seen the inside of a gym ever, when a knock sounded at the door. It had to be Krissy or Savior and I put my money on the latter since the former didn't have enough competence to find my address. If she did, I'm sure I would have received a visit by now. My day had already been long and shitty, and I was in no mood for visitors.

I felt steam coming off my body at the sight of Savior. "What do you want?"

"For starters, to come in."

I didn't feel like arguing so I stepped back and let him in, waiting for him to speak his peace.

"Well?"

His gaze tracked over my body, heating me up against my will.

"I uhm, wanted to ..." he trailed off, but those blue eyes wandered over my legs, the swell of my breasts, my lips.

In that moment I knew what this was about. All these unexpected visits. The anger.

"Fine. That's what you want, Savior? I'm in."

I could use a good hard fuck after the day I'd had anyway. I kept my gaze trained on his, soaking up those sapphire eyes and the need I saw in them as I pulled the racerback tank over my head.

"Let's do this."

I knew he'd deny why he showed up and I didn't feel like talking anymore, so I took a few steps forward and fisted his shirt in my hands, pulling him down until our lips clashed.

He resisted at first, like I knew he would. But seconds later his lips relaxed and his hands went to my ass and squeezed, pulling me closer. His lips were especially soft against the rough scruff of his beard, drawing memories to the forefront that I'd chosen to forget.

"Mandy," he grunted when I pulled back.

"Savior," I shot back with a smile as I shimmied out of the tight black pants, kicking them aside until I was completely naked. I stood there with my hands on my hips, daring him to come closer or walk away. I was prepared for either option, but he closed the gap between us and grabbed my breasts in his big hands.

"Fuck me, Mandy."

"That's what I'm trying to do," I told him seriously. "Fuck," I bit out when he leaned forward and slicked his tongue over my nipple before pulling it into his mouth. My head dropped back and my hands shot to his hair, fingers curling around the thick locks. "Savior," I groaned again. His mouth was magic and fierce, lighting my fire from deep within and he kept it stoked for several long minutes as his tongue, his lips, traveled up and down my body.

"Mandy," he growled and pressed me up against the nearest wall, I turned to give him my back, arching slowly.

"Like this." I didn't want to look at him, didn't want to peer up into those blue eyes that shifted colors with the changing of his desire, his passion. I just wanted him to fill me up, make me come and forget about everything else. A low growl sounded behind me, along with the swish of a zipper and the sound of a condom wrapper opening.

He entered in one hard thrust that sent shivers rocketing through my body, flames burned up my already overheated flesh. He was long and thick, and from this position *he* was all I could feel. Everywhere.

"Yes!"

Hands braced on the wall, I pushed back with every thrust, hungry to have every inch of him buried deep inside me. Pounding into me. "Fuck," I grunted when he grabbed my hips and slammed deep. Harder and harder, fast and rough. "More!"

One hand gripped the back of my neck and I arched my back, sending him deeper.

"Fuck, Mandy. You're so goddamn tight."

"Shut up and fuck me." I didn't want words, just action so I pushed back and he froze. Something changed deep inside Savior and he moved in closer so his body molded against the back of mine. One hand on my hip and the other moved to my breast, squeezing hard as he pounded his cock deep into me over and over again. Thick and hard, he filled me, so thick and delicious as his teeth sank into the crook of my neck.

"Yes!"

My orgasm was just out of reach but when Savior pinched my nipple, that was the magic switch that unleashed the floodgates.

"Oh fuck … yes!" My whole body trembled violently as the orgasm wound its way through my veins before exploding out of my pores. The tiny tremors gripped him hard and pumped his cock until his own orgasm exploded.

"Fuck! Shit!" he roared in my ear, pounding hard and deep, his body pressing me into the wall as the orgasm shot out of him. He stilled, and then swiped his tongue across the back of my neck until I shivered.

"Mandy."

I bit back a moan as our bodies separated, turning to him with a smile.

"Thanks." That was the perfect way to end such a shitty day.

But apparently Savior didn't appreciate my gratitude. "What?"

"Thanks," I told him and placed a friendly hand on his shoulder. "Don't worry, Savior. That was great but I'm not expecting anything, so you don't need to make up an excuse about why you need to leave and you can spare me your guilt and regret."

He stood there, looking delicious with his tattooed chest, six pack abs and still hard cock pointing in my direction. But he was angry. "Is this some type of fucking payback?"

I laughed but there was no humor in it. "Of course not. It was a really hot, hard fuck. It was … just what I needed."

"Why me?"

I shrugged. "Why not? What other reason would you keep showing up at my job, my apartment?"

DELICIOUSLY DAMAGED

He grunted and yanked his jeans and underwear off the floor. "Like I said before, to clear the goddamn air!"

"And I told *you* that there was no air to clear! But of course, you know better what I need and how I feel than I do, right?"

Disgusted, I picked up my clothes and walked across the room before turning back to him. "You can clean up, but then you need to leave." The glow of my orgasm faded quickly and now I just felt sore and pissed off as I kicked my bedroom door shut and put my clothes on. Dropping down on the bed, I closed my eyes and listened as Savior moved around my apartment. Water running in the bathroom, his heavy footsteps on the floor and then the sound of the door closing as he left.

When I was sure he was gone, I locked the door and crashed on the bed. Even something as simple as uncomplicated as casual pleasure found a way of turning fucked up and complicated.

Maybe I just needed to invest in a really good vibrator.

Chapter 6

Savior

Fucking women. Even if I lived to be ten thousand fucking years old, I'd never fucking understand them or how their brains worked. And Mandy went to the top of that damn list. I was furious, so pissed off with her, but every time I thought about *why*, about fucking her hard and fast up against that wall while she urged me on with dirty, passion-filled words, my cock sprang to life. Ready for a repeat performance.

But that wouldn't happen. It shouldn't have happened the first time and contrary to what she thought, I didn't go there to fuck her. But how could I resist her, standing there all proud and strong, her gorgeous tits on display as she stepped in closer to me? I was just a man and goddammit, I couldn't resist her. So I'd have to keep my distance.

If only I could.

Mandy was part of the Reckless Bastards family whether she wanted to be or not. Ammo was one of us, had always been one of us, and that meant she would always be one of us. Which is how I found myself parking my bike beside her little sedan and stomping up the steps to her apartment door, chipped with green paint, again. I knocked and waited, prepared for just about any response from her at this point. I'd be just as surprised to get a kick to the dick as a blowjob.

She opened the door and her green eyes narrowed as she looked me over from head to toe.

"Not interested."

She stepped back and slammed the door but I caught the flimsy piece of wood easily. She stepped back, looking bored rather than scared.

"You said I don't know you, don't know shit about your life over the past few years and you were right." I stepped inside and kicked her door shut. "Tell me."

"No."

DELICIOUSLY DAMAGED

I knew she wouldn't be easy, but she had no idea how stubborn I could be if set my mind to it.

"Come on, tell me."

I brushed past her and sat on the sofa, kicking my boots up and getting comfortable. The more she glared, the brighter my smile became.

"You hungry? I'll order some pizza and wings. No, fuck wings, let's get those spicy boneless things."

I pulled out my phone and pulled up my favorite pizza place.

"Address," I said, snapping my fingers at her and risking the health of my balls and my brain.

She rattled it off and then tossed a pillow at my head. "Jackass."

"We've got about forty minutes until the food arrives, so why don't you burn some calories by flapping that jaw?"

I dropped back down and crossed my legs on her wooden coffee table, while she glared a hole in the side of my head.

"Why are you doing this?" She stepped over my legs, giving me plenty of time to stare at her shapely legs.

"Seriously. What could you possibly get out of this?"

"I get a chance to fill a hole in my education, namely what you've been up to since I last saw you."

She stared, eyes all squinty and hard, but the way her hair stood up straight everywhere lessened the effect.

"Why don't you stop trying to figure out my motives and just tell me?"

Mandy was a stubborn thing, but she had nothing on me.

"Nothing to tell, really. I worked and then I hopped on a bus headed for the east coast. A little while later I started culinary school."

DELICIOUSLY DAMAGED

"Did you always want to be a chef?"

I realized I knew nothing about her, aside from those care packages she used to send Ammo. "I knew you baked one hell of a cookie but Ammo never said you wanted to do it professionally."

She shrugged but I saw the smile tug on the corners of her pouty mouth.

"I never really thought about it, but things weren't how I wanted them to be here and I knew I had to get away before it was too late. I went to the library and applied for scholarships, but after taking an online aptitude test that said I could run a kitchen, that's what I decided to do."

She tried to make light of it, but I could tell it meant something to her.

"You love it."

This time her smile was genuine as she nodded.

"I do. Food makes people happy and so does art, I get to do both every day."

"The food you made for the engagement party was delicious. Best triple chocolate chunk cupcakes ever."

A blush spread over her pale skin.

"Yeah, thanks."

"What did you mean you had to get away before it was too late?" Her shoulders slumped, like I could forget something like that. The doorbell rang and she hopped up with a smile.

"I'll get that," she said, relief in her voice.

"I already paid," I told her and smiled at the growl she let out. It was kind of sexy. I never had a woman growl at me before. Just like that my mind went to all the ways I could make Mandy growl some more.

"Did you invite people over?"

"No, why?"

Green eyes bugged way out, clearly telling me that I was an idiot, but again, the effect was ruined by her hair standing up everywhere.

"Because this is enough food for at least ten people, Savior."

She set the box and the foam container on the table and disappeared into the kitchen.

"I don't know what you were thinking."

She returned with two plates and two beers.

"I was thinking that ten years is a long time to cover and we might get hungry walking down Memory Lane."

She rolled her eyes. "You are so full of shit, you know that?"

Her words caught me off guard. "Damn, how many times did Ammo say that to me over the years?"

Just the way she had with a mix of incredulity and affection.

"Too many," she agreed.

"So?" I dropped a slice onto both plates and waited for her to answer. "You gonna tell me what you did here that made you need to escape?"

She shook her head as she chewed. Her body language was casual and easy but a hard glint had returned to her eyes.

"Now you care? I seem to remember Ammo telling me, no *promising* me that if I needed anything to call you or *the club*," she scoffed, shooting me finger quotes and rolling her eyes to show her disdain. "A lot of good that did me when you didn't answer calls or stop in to check on me."

I wanted to shout that she was wrong, but she wasn't. We'd dropped the ball where she was concerned and now unease settled low in my gut like a ball of lead as I imagined the worst shit she could've gotten up to as a girl in sin city. But I needed to know. "So?"

"So you don't get to know, Savior." She shook her head like she was explaining something simple to an idiot. "You had a chance to know and you didn't care. I did what I had to in order to survive, and I did. But that's the past."

DELICIOUSLY DAMAGED

I didn't like it. Not one fucking bit, but I also knew she was right. I would let her hang on to her secrets, for now, but not for long. "Does how you survived have anything to do with those assholes in the parking lot?"

She nodded and nibbled her lip, her eyes dancing all around the living room, everywhere but at me. I knew she could feel the weight of my stare on her, mostly because less than two feet separated us, but also because I could see the pink stain on her skin and the way her pulse fluttered in her neck. "This chick I knew back then helped me get an I.D. so that I could . . ."

She paused and I thought I might have lost her but she picked up her story again.

". . . take care of myself," she said vaguely. Now that I'm back she wants me to do one more job for her and I won't do it. Those assholes were trying to convince me to change my mind."

Fuck, that was a lot worse than I thought. The guilt piled on top of my fear. We should have been there for her. If it had been any of us, Ammo would have barged in and made sure she had healthy fucking meals and did her homework. He would have been there in all the ways we hadn't been for her. I knew what women did to survive in Vegas, hell all around the world, and the thought she might have done that, made me sick to my stomach. Made my skin burn with anger. "You got more beer?"

She stood like she hadn't just dropped a major fucking bomb that had my head spinning.

"Unlikely. Those two were a fluke," she said as she disappeared into the kitchen again. "I have vodka and I have rum. There's probably tequila in the freezer but you can't have that. It's mine."

That pulled a laugh from me. "Stingy with your booze, Mandy?"

"Your guilt doesn't deserve tequila. It gets rum or vodka, take your pick." She held a bottle in each hand but my gaze was drawn to the stiff peaks of her nipples poking through the fabric of her shirt. My mouth watered.

"Fine, I'll take the vodka."

DELICIOUSLY DAMAGED

She sat on the floor across from me and grinned as she set the bottle and two tumblers on the table, haphazardly pouring odd amounts in each glass. "The first shot is the numbing agent."

I eyed the so-called shot skeptically. "That's at least two shots."

"Okay booze police, drink what you can. Grandpa."

Fuck that. I lifted the glass to my lips and let the cool liquid burn my insides. "At least it's the good shit. Now, tell me what you did to survive."

She grinned, the first genuine smile I'd seen from her in a long damn time. "Wouldn't you like to know?"

"I would," I told her seriously but she only grinned wider.

"First, you don't get to know. Second, I'm not drunk enough to spill by accident." She knocked back her shot and poured another as she reached for the spicy chicken. "Thanks to all this food, I'll never be."

"Oh don't you worry about that sweetheart, I've gotten many a woman drunk in my day." It would tease all of my patience to get her drunk and not fuck her again, but I was determined to do just that.

Secrets, yes. Sex, no.

I had this.

Chapter 7

Mandy

I couldn't believe it. I was having a good time with Savior. A man who could be pretty damn charming when he wasn't waking up with a big bag of regret. I found myself laughing more than I had in far too long. It was probably the vodka. Okay it was mostly the vodka, but it was also him. In my mind, Savior was still the unreliable man who'd ditched me the minute he'd gotten stateside and couldn't be bothered with the boring details of being a teenager. That wasn't him any more than the card-counting delinquent was still me.

I let the vodka do its thing, let it relax my mind and my body until the *awkward* disappeared and all that was left were two people connected by their memories and grief of the same person.

"He would be so thrilled with all the businesses you guys have." Ammo was proud of the Reckless Bastards and to see them thriving the way Savior described, I could admit a certain warmth blossomed in my chest.

He grinned in that way he had that made him look almost like a boy. No, not a boy but just a man who didn't have ghosts, demons. Skeletons. His eyes were clear and his smile wide. "We have Ammo O.G. that we grow ourselves. It's our biggest seller, especially 'cause it's some kick ass weed."

Now that would have tickled my brother like crazy. "I wish he could've seen that."

I could see Ammo strutting around in what passed for heaven for guys like him, bragging about being a celebrity. It'd been a long time since I could think of my brother without sadness. Pouring the last of the vodka in our glasses, I held it up.

"To the best brother around. May he be shocking angels and heathens alike, wherever he is."

"Damn straight," Savior said and knocked the vodka back with a grimace. "It's good to remember. Sometimes I forget it all. It's easier."

DELICIOUSLY DAMAGED

I sighed, nodding. "Most of the time I wish I could. I tried forgetting but now that it's only me, I have to remember. If I ever have a family, they'll want to know about how well my mom sang or how my dad did the best card tricks. They won't know the dirty jokes that Ammo horrified me with when I was too young to hear them. So, I remember."

For an uncertain future I wasn't sure I even wanted.

"Are you drunk enough to spill your secrets yet?"

Just the sound of his voice, so deep and rumbly, made me smile. But a moment later as his question sank in, I felt the smile fade.

"No offense, but I'll never be drunk enough for that." It wasn't a big secret, but it was mine and he'd given up the right to ask.

"Come on, how bad could it be? Prostitution?"

I laughed bitterly. "Yeah, right. If I'd done that we might have actually crossed paths back then." It was no secret that the Reckless Bastards had been in on the ass business well before it became fashionable. With it now legal*ish*, I was sure they made bank.

"That's a fucking relief." He smacked the sofa as his body sank deeper into it. "If it's not that, just tell me." He was insistent and the more he drank the more his guilt showed. Now that he knew I hadn't been out there putting a price tag on my body, his guilt seemed to lessen, but not by much.

Good. He should feel guilty. I didn't want him carrying some burden, but he and all the Reckless Bastards had let me down.

"Look Savior, I don't need you to feel guilty for not keeping your promise to Ammo. I'm sure he wouldn't either because everything turned out fine. Just drop it."

"I really am sorry. There's no excuse and I'm grateful I'll never get the ass kicking I deserve from Ammo."

"Don't think you're going to heaven?"

He laughed. "Sweetheart if I make it up there he can kick my ass daily."

"At any rate, I don't need your guilt so get over yourself."

"Then why don't you want anything to do with us?"

I shook my head. "Because I'm still not your responsibility. And even if you or any of the other Bastards *think* otherwise, I wouldn't trust you to have my back anyway."

"Damn."

That one word held so much emotion, like a perfect bite of food. He was shocked, hurt even.

"You don't pull any punches."

"Well, you won't stop pushing. Now you know what the deal is, you don't have to keep checking up on me. I've learned how to take care of myself over the years."

His dark brows rose suspiciously. "Even those goons from the parking lot?"

"They're not the first goons I've come across." But with any luck, they would be the last. Goons were all fine and good in the movies, in real life they were a lot dumber and ten times as dangerous. "Like I said, I can take care of myself."

Savior tried to stand and stumbled. Since it was the first time he stood in hours it was clear he was drunker than he thought.

"Shit."

He wobbled and pointed at me. "For the record sweet Mandy, I don't do shit I don't want to do."

Savior dropped back down onto my sofa and I stood, scanning the room for a bucket even though I was pretty sure I didn't have a bucket at all.

"Fine. Just lie down and don't puke on my shit." I pushed him onto his back and went to pour a cup of water. "Drink this."

"I'm fine. Not the first time I've been drunk before, tough ass."

DELICIOUSLY DAMAGED

I laughed and took off his ridiculously heavy motorcycle boots. At least I assumed they were the real article, but they could just as easily be a fashion statement.

"I'm not surprised but unlike your tree house, I care if you get puke all over my stuff."

"Club house."

"What?" He couldn't be that drunk, could he? Not when I only had a nice buzz going.

"It's a club house not a fucking tree house. We're men, not elves."

My whole body shook with laughter. "I don't know, Savior, your club shares plenty of similarities with elves. The only real difference is your size."

One eye popped open, as blue as the sky. "Am I that drunk or did you seriously just compare my club to elves?"

"Both of those things are true, old man. You can sleep on the sofa until you're sober enough to drive home." I grabbed his chin until he opened both eyes and yeah, he was beautiful but that wasn't the point. "But I don't need you to check up on me, okay?"

He nodded and as I stepped back two big arms wrapped around me and pulled me down onto him.

"You talk too much," he said and then speared both hands through my short hair and kissed me like I was his favorite brand of biker whiskey.

I should have pulled back, but I didn't. I couldn't. He tasted too good, felt too fucking good with his hard body pressed up against mine. I wished we were naked because he was growing harder by the second and my body was hot, wet and ready. But we weren't doing that. Fuck.

"That's a novel way to shut someone up."

He flashed a lazy grin, his eyes still closed as his thumb brushed my jaw. "I check up on you because I want to. I fucked you because you're hot and I will fuck you again," he grinned but it was softer, and I knew he was seconds from passing out. "And again."

I slid off his body as soon as his deep, even breaths sounded. Grabbing the debris from the table and putting it away before I closed myself up in my bedroom. I slid into the bed and clenched my knees tight beneath my comforter as I drifted off to sleep, telling my body not to think or dream about the big, blue-eyed devil asleep on my sofa.

Yeah, sometimes my body could be a real bitch.

***

"You want time off?" Landry's voice bellowed just as he meant it to. He loved to draw attention whenever he could, but especially when he wanted to humiliate someone. It was how he got his chubby little cock hard.

"I'm asking for next *Saturday* off, yes." With my arms crossed, I stood with a blank expression on my face and waited for him to respond.

"Get a load of hot shit Sutton, guys. She wants Saturday off, our busiest day." He laughed, clutching his swollen gut as his dark eyes glared at me. "Do you have a fancy Hollywood party to go to where you pretend you and only you are responsible for the delicious confections that come out of my kitchen?"

"Since this is Las Vegas, no, no Hollywood party." The rest of that statement didn't warrant a response. Though Vegas had its own over the top culinary flair, Landry pretended like this was New York in the eighties. The only cutthroat person around was him, but his toxic personality turned the culinary press against him. And he was powerless to change it because he saw himself as flawless.

"I hear Dinah and Dean have booked a table for Saturday, I should call and let them know it's not my dessert they'll be eating," I said.

"Absolutely not! Worried they'll like my food better than yours?" he taunted like the sniveling little shit bastard he was. "Let's see what they have to say." Meaning he would lay the blame on me when they hated it.

DELICIOUSLY DAMAGED

"Sure," I told him easily because the truth was, one of their production assistants had already called and I let it slip. Totally accidentally, of course. "So, next Saturday?"

He was already distracted, probably thinking of all the desserts he could fuck up and blame on me. "Yeah, sure. Take it off."

I turned on my heels with a smile, walking away quickly before he remembered he changed his mind. My shift was over and I was ready to go home and put my feet up. Landry had me come in early to help with egg whites but I knew he really wanted to punish me for getting another mention from a critic. It was nice, but none of it really mattered because when I left *Knead* for good, I'd still need a recommendation from Landry.

I stopped just inside the exit to send a quick text to Teddy, letting her know she could count me among the guests for Jana and Max's upcoming wedding. Now I had to find a dress and shoes and all that other crap that went along with dressing up, since the last time I dressed up it was to put my brother's body in the ground. I wasn't about to wear a funeral dress to a wedding.

The temperature had been in the high eighties all day, making the kitchen even hotter than the ten million ovens going at once. Now that the sun was so close to the horizon, the weather and the view was just about perfect. The light breeze whipped through my red V-neck tee, cooling my damp skin underneath. Cool air smacked against my nipples and just like that, I was back there, the night I buried Ammo, with Savior's mouth closed around one stiff peak, staring at me with that wicked smile I couldn't resist. Especially not in the thick of my grief over losing my older brother. My protector.

Even in my haze I made it to my car without being assaulted or accosted by anyone. Then a fucking brick came sailing through the back window, luckily, on the passenger side.

"Son of a bitch!"

DELICIOUSLY DAMAGED

I looked over my shoulder just in time to see some asshole in a hoodie running away. I didn't know who it was, but I knew what he wanted.

To send a message.

Yeah, yeah. They wanted my skill at counting cards. I got it. Too bad they couldn't have it. I put the car in drive and made my way home. I still hadn't figured out what to do about Krissy and her thugs, but I would. And then this shit would stop.

"Hey, Mandy!"

I froze at the unfamiliar voice, clutching my keys between my fingers as I turned and stepped back.

"Oh, shit, Teddy. What's up?"

"Not as enthusiastic as I was hoping for, but we'll work on it. Shopping. I figured you probably wanted to do some shopping for San Diego and I came as support."

"Who said I needed support?"

"Oh please. We both know you'll go into the first boutique you find, grab something black or maybe plain blue you can wear again and again. I can help without taking all day."

I was still skeptical. I liked Teddy just fine, yet, the last thing I wanted was to spend more time shopping.

Then, she sweetened the offer. "I'll buy you a burger and a beer after."

One look at her welcoming smile and my resistance melted in the Vegas sun. "Sold."

She flashed a satisfied grin. "Good. I'll wait until you've had a drink or two before I ask you what the hell happened to your window." I groaned and she just laughed. "I'll even let you take a shower first."

"Wow, Teddy, and they say models are mean."

She laughed at my deadpan delivery. "I'm a *former* model so maybe I'm losing my edge."

"Yeah, right. You're the type of chick born with an edge." She was confident and tough, beautiful but not all in your face about it.

DELICIOUSLY DAMAGED

"Nah. Trust me, it was hard earned."

There was a story there but we didn't know each other well enough to share those kinds of secrets. She got in her car, followed me home and I welcomed her inside my apartment. "Now go get clean," she said, "and I'll wait out here."

"Sure," I said uncertainly as she began to look at my few books and pictures.

It didn't take me long to scrub the kitchen stink off me and it had very little to do with the fact that Teddy was wandering loose inside my apartment. I didn't waste time in the shower, ever.

"Don't worry, I didn't snoop," she assured me when I returned to the living room. "I prefer to pry the info from my prey."

The gleam in her eyes would've frightened me if there were anything remotely interesting about me. "You'd be disappointed."

"Somehow I doubt that. Especially considering the energy I saw zapping between you and Savior."

I shook my head. "Don't even think about it. There's nothing there and there's nothing interesting about me."

"I'll be the judge of that."

I guessed this was what I got for wanting friends.

Chapter 8

Savior

"You're an old fucker if you need a pee break again. We're practically back in Mayhem now," I chortled, setting the stand on my bike and reaching for the gas nozzle.

Max glared at me and I just laughed back at him. He damn near ripped the cap off the bottle of water, probably imagining it was my head.

We were on our way back from a gun show just outside Reno, but the prospects had probably already made it back to the clubhouse with the guns.

"Fuck you, it's ten thousand goddamn degrees out here." He chugged one bottle before he stomped inside the gas station and came back out with two more bottles. "Too fucking hot!"

"Relax and drink your water. I won't tell Jana she's marrying a senior citizen as long as you promise to be generous with those early bird specials." I laughed again when he flipped me off. "You ready to get married, man?"

Max's face softened, setting the bottled on his saddle. "Fuck yeah. I mean, me and Jana are solid. I can't wait to make her mine, you know? She saved my life, wouldn't let me get lost in my bullshit."

His smile was so genuine, so sincere it brought up a memory I hadn't thought about in too long. The last time I saw my mother.

I was eleven and Mom was crying, thick black mascara or maybe it was eyeliner streamed down her cheeks, so she looked like the mess she was. Her latest loser du jour had threatened to leave because he hadn't signed on "to be saddled with a brat."

Strong words from a man who sat in his underwear all day before sneaking out after midnight to play pool and sell dope.

She was filled with tears and a genuine horror I'd never seen before. The thought of that asshole — Cal was his name — leaving had her so filled with fear she could barely form words. Then it got worse. She begged. On her goddamn knees, she begged that fucker not to leave her. And he looked at me with a gleam in his eyes and drew one side of his mouth up in a snarl and told her simply: "It's him or me."

I knew my fate before she even turned to look at me. Her eyes pleading with me to understand. I knew she wanted me to give her some sign it was okay to choose that prick over me. Even at eleven I was a stubborn little shit. I didn't want her to go with him or to leave me, but even as a kid I knew I couldn't let her see it. I couldn't let her or Cal see that weakness.

I went to my room and when I came out the next morning, they were both gone. No note or memento, just a coffee can with three hundred and forty-six dollars and two rolls of quarters.

"Damn man, where'd you go?"

Max's voice pulled me from memories best left buried. "Some different variation of hell."

"No shit," he commiserated. Max was all fucked up with PTSD when he came to Mayhem looking for his brother, but with the help of a head shrinker and a hot little blonde, the man was weeks away from getting married. "Never goes away, but when the day ends and there are more good memories than bad, it's a good fucking day."

That was about all most of us could hope for. More good than bad, because there was no fucking chance the memories went away. They sometimes hid for a while, took a break until you thought that shit was behind you, then they crept up on you like a fucking sniper's bullet. "Waking up to a beautiful woman doesn't hurt."

"Definitely doesn't." He flashed a satisfied grin. "What's up with you and Mandy?"

"Nothing. Why do you ask?" He grinned like he knew something but Mandy didn't strike me as the girl talk kind of woman.

DELICIOUSLY DAMAGED

"I overheard Jana and Teddy talking. Teddy says something definitely happened between you two," he said, his gaze too damn studious for my liking.

"Nothing did."

"Since the funeral," he finally added.

"Smug prick." A laugh roared out of him, startling the young couple in the VW bug at the air pump.

"So, you fucked her after her brother's funeral and then you told her it was a huge mistake, is that about right?"

I nodded.

"Then I left town and I hadn't seen her until she showed up at the clubhouse last month." Shit, had it already been a month? Why the fuck was I counting?

"And in the last month you've been reading the Bible together?"

I laughed. "Well we've both spent time on our knees."

"So, Teddy was right? Do you like her or are you just getting your dick wet?"

"Does it matter?"

We had rules in the club, but we also didn't get all up in each other's personal business unless it interfered with club business.

"No, I'm just curious."

That pulled another laugh out of me. "When did you become such a gossip?"

He shrugged and got back on his bike. "It's fucking Jana and Teddy. No, it's women. They have this way of making everything sound like shit you just have to hear. And the worst part? It's always juicy gossip, about people I don't fucking know!"

I laughed and kicked my engine into gear. "You domesticated pussy."

He flipped me off with another laugh as he mounted his own bike. "Yeah, but I go to sleep and wake up with a warm, sexy woman in my arms. Half the time she makes me breakfast."

DELICIOUSLY DAMAGED

"And the other half?"

"She makes it *for* me," he said with a smug grin and took off, leaving me to catch up with his crazy ass.

We were only about a hundred miles from home; I used that time to clear my head, even though Max's words kept playing in my head. The way he looked when he talked about Jana and their future was a far cry from the shell-shocked half a person he'd been when he first got here. I was happy for him, but that future wasn't for me.

When we made it back to the clubhouse, Max stomped over to me looking as serious as I'd seen him in a long time.

"I got sidetracked by that fucking gossip," he grumbled and raked a hand through his hair. "Teddy said someone busted Mandy's window out. She was cagey about it, said it was random but Teddy didn't believe her."

I knew who'd done it, even if I didn't know their names. Yet. "Thanks, Max."

"She all right?"

"She will be. Let's go handle our business so you can get home to your woman."

That stubborn woman was enough to drive a man to drink, and I was already a drinkin' man.

***

"So, you are alive," I said as soon as Mandy opened the door, looking good enough to eat in short pink shorts and tight white top that cupped her tits perfectly. One little bead of sweat trickled down her jaw to her neck, making a straight line down her chest and between the little shadowed spot between her breasts. Fucking delectable.

"Have you heard otherwise?"

"Always the smartass. I wasn't sure, since you've been doing a pretty good job of ignoring me."

She rolled her eyes and walked away, giving me a long look at the sweet curve of her ass. Firm but meaty, enough to hold on to when the fucking got way too good.

"I didn't realize you were looking for me."

"Even with that pretty little face of yours honey, you ain't sellin' innocent."

She shrugged and grinned. "It was worth a shot. Look, I told you I don't need you checking up on me and I figured Teddy told you about my window and you were coming around to He-Man someone over it."

I laughed. "With these good looks, I'm more of a Batman." She wasn't far off the mark otherwise though. "Who says I didn't come for sex?"

"Did you?"

Her nipples poked through the tank top and my mouth watered because I knew she had a bra on; the blue cotton peeked over the swell of her cleavage.

She was turned on by my suggestion. "Would that be all right?"

She shrugged. "Other than the fact it would be a massive mistake? Hell yeah." She stood, half eager and half hesitating before her shoulders fell. "What are you doing here, Savior?"

"Did you get your window fixed?"

"Yes."

"Are you going to the wedding?" She nodded and I had to clamp my teeth together to stop from screaming at her stubborn ass.

"I am."

"Did you make sure you got a room at the hotel with us?" I knew she was perfectly capable of taking care of herself, because it was like her fucking mantra, never wanting anyone's help. But San Diego was a tourist town and she was a petite woman who stood no chance against a strong, determined man.

"No. I'm coming the day of the wedding and leaving that night."

"Fuck no."

She took a step back. "Excuse me? Who do you think you are?"

"I don't want to hear it, Mandy. You're not driving all that way, not alone. I'll pick you up."

Why the fuck was I being so high handed with her?

"Go to hell, Savior. I'm not your kid, not your sister and I am *not* your responsibility!"

She began to push at me with everything she had, which was a lot, but we both knew I only moved because I wanted to. "Get out and go find someone else to babysit and harass!"

"But you're my favorite person to harass," I told her with a wry grin.

"Go away," she groaned but I could see the way her lips twitched, like she was hiding her smile. "I'll see you around."

"You will. I'll pick you up at nine on Thursday morning. Don't be late." She grunted at me and continued to push me toward the door. When we were close I flipped our positions and pressed her against the door, pushing my body against her enough to make her react but not enough to hurt. "Got it?"

She looked up at me and those icy green eyes darkened to jade to go along with that sexy gasp she couldn't stop if she wanted to.

"Don't tell me what to do."

Her voice was husky because she couldn't control how her body responded to me, but she meant what she said.

"Damn you're so fucking frustrating." Her eyes lit with mischief as my mouth crashed down on hers, devouring the sweet lemony flavor on her tongue, the soft slick of her plump lips against mine. The way her fingers looped through my waistband possessively sent all the blood in my body straight to my cock. Her small, wiry arms wrapped around my neck and she jumped into my arms, wrapped her legs around my waist so her hot pussy was right where I wanted it. I squeezed her ass and she sucked on my tongue, moaning from deep in her belly.

DELICIOUSLY DAMAGED

She felt so good in my arms that I wished we were both naked, so I could thrust deep, impale her on my cock. And I knew she'd let me and she wouldn't even be self-conscious about being all sweaty from working out or cleaning. I didn't care, in fact I liked her like this. My mouth watered to taste more of her. She pulled back, her eyes hazy with desire. Slowly surprise took over.

"You . . . you are dangerous. I'll see you when I get to San Diego, Savior. Not before."

She pointed a finger at me. I bit it.

"Stop that."

"I'll let you think about that kiss for the next few days. And then I'll see you bright and early Thursday morning, sweetheart."

I let her slide down my body, gritting my teeth the entire time to keep from taking what we both wanted.

"Do what you want and I'll do the same."

Mandy and her smart mouth were gonna get her in trouble. "Don't test me, Mandy."

"Don't boss me around, Savior."

Damn she was hot when she got all pissed off, which she did a lot.

"Nine o'clock." I pulled the door open and walked through it. "Lock the door."

She muttered angrily from the other side of the door and I smiled, wondering if her skin was all flushed like it was when she got pissed off. If her nipples were tight little beads. But still, the door didn't lock.

"Mandy." I gave her one full minute. A full fucking minute and still she didn't lock the door, not even the one inside the knob. I pushed the door open and watched her eyes light with surprise as I pushed her into the wall with my body.

"What do you think you're doing?"

"What you wanted when you decided not to lock the fucking door."

I dipped my hand into the waistband of her shorts, past the small scrap of cotton and right into the dripping nectar between her thighs.

"So fucking wet."

I slid my finger deep until it was coated. She pulsed around me as I pulled it out and we both groaned.

She watched, with her lips slightly parted as I put that finger in my mouth and sucked it clean. Mandy choked on a gasp and then licked her lips in desire. "You came back just for that?"

"I'll get the rest Thursday. Now, lock the fuckin' door."

"Bossy," she muttered, but she flipped the locks and I walked away with a hardon and a smile.

KB WINTERS

Chapter 9

Mandy

I had everything I needed for the four plus hour drive to San Diego. I made éclairs last night for the road, packed my bags and woke up in plenty of time to pack and be gone a full hour before Savior darkened my doorstep. I hadn't planned on spending the entire weekend with the Reckless Bastards, since they weren't really my friends, but I knew Savior would show up today and force the issue, so I had to get up and get that worm before he swooped in and stole it from me. It was ten minutes to eight and everything was all set. I pulled the door open, arms laden with snacks and my purse, and slammed into a tall, blue-eyed biker wearing a smug grin offering me coffee and a grease-stained bag of pastries.

"Trying to sneak off to San Diego without me?" He shocked the hell out of me and moved inside, kicking the door shut before I could recover my senses.

But with his man-scent enveloping me in the tiny apartment, that was harder to do.

"I wasn't *sneaking* anywhere, just leaving. For *my* trip. To San Diego."

I could admit, only to myself, that I was impressed he'd caught on to my plan and foiled it, but I wasn't happy.

"At least I got a cronut out of the deal," I told him, picking out the sweet pastry from the selection in the bag before taking a less than ladylike bite. It was from my favorite bakery. Was he a mind reader, too? "It's a little sweet for my taste but it'll give me the energy rush I need for the drive ahead of me."

He smirked. "It's not that long, especially since I'm driving. Both of us."

"If you mean you and your gigantic ego, then I agree. But if I'm part of that equation, you should probably stop smoking crack."

His laugh boomed loud in the quiet room so early in the morning.

"Why are you being so stubborn when we both know I could convince you? Easily."

I laughed to hide the truth. He could convince me if he set his mind to it, but I wouldn't let it get that far. I hoped I wouldn't.

"Look Savior, I appreciate the pastry but I'm full up on bossy men, so I'll see you around. Hey, what the hell are you doing?"

He stole my cronut and tossed it back in the bag and set it on the table next to my purse and the coffee he'd brought.

"I'm going to convince you that we could be the perfect road trip buddies." He'd tossed me over his shoulder, and I heard the mischief and desire in the playful nature of his voice. I yelped when he smacked my ass, biting my lip to keep the moan from escaping.

He tossed me on the bed with a dark, hungry look I chose to ignore for the sake of my sanity.

"I don't need convincing Savior and I damn sure don't need you to watch over me."

He peeled my sneakers off, letting his hands glide up the legs I'd chosen to keep bare in a lightweight cotton dress for the long, hot drive.

"Mandy, sweetheart, I ain't trying to watch over you."

His fingertips kneaded my thighs, gliding up until his thumbs brushed where I was already drenched and throbbing. For him.

"I'm trying to watch you come. You look so fucking hot when you come."

He didn't wait for my acquiescence or my submission, he just stared for a long tense moment and then it was like someone flipped a switch because he moved like a tornado, taking off my panties, my dress and my bra.

"So goddamn delicious!"

I shivered at his words, at the hungry look in his eyes and the possessive way he touched me. It was hard not to feel special, desired when a man like Savior looked at me like that.

DELICIOUSLY DAMAGED

And then his mouth was on my neck, the weight of his body pressed into mine, so wicked and so hot. His mouth moved with the precision of a skilled lover across my neck, scraping against my collarbone before he moved down to the valley between my breasts.

He nibbled at the soft flesh around my nipples before sucking it deep into his mouth, making me tremble at the hot friction between them.

"Savior."

His name escaped, unbidden as the pressure building deep inside me.

He said nothing, just savored my breasts, licking and sucking, nibbling and biting. The switch from rough to gentle, soft to hard, it was too much. He'd barely touched me and I could already feel my orgasm building. When his hand slid down my belly and two thick fingers slipped inside me just as he blew against my aching nipple before wrapping his mouth around it, I fell apart with his name on my tongue. Again.

"Shit babe, you're so wet."

"Your handiwork," I told him with a lazy chuckle.

"Now I need to see how sweet you taste, how thick that sweet cream of yours is on my tongue."

I didn't know how he said the dirty things he did with such ease, but his words never failed to get a rise out of me.

"Unless you're convinced?"

I shrugged. "I'm totally convinced that I'm driving my car to San Diego," I told him with a laugh but his tongue slipped between my pussy lips, licking me from the bottom of my opening all the way up to my swollen clit.

"Fuck, Savior, yes."

I gripped his thick brown hair around my fingers and arched into him as his tongue devoured me. He grunted and growled, animalistic in his desire for me and I knew, this wasn't about convincing me to ride with him to San Diego. This was about him and me.

I couldn't be mad at him or his controlling alpha ways, not when he had me flat on my back with his face buried between my legs like his only goal in life was to make me come. The rough friction of his beard against my thighs added a tantalizing sensation that was hard to describe. To make my pussy so drenched, so tight and greedy that I couldn't get close enough, couldn't feel enough of him. I don't think any of the men I'd been with had ever paid such close attention to me or my pleasure, not the way Savior just stayed down there, noting every little reaction from me, adjusting his movements to maximize my pleasure.

"Savior," I warned him as my body clenched tight. His tongue went wild, sliding figure eights around my clit as his thumb slipped just inside me and flung me off the edge of the proverbial cliff and right into some headlong, dizzying pleasure that I could barely stand.

"Oh fuck! Shit . . . yes!"

My body trembled and convulsed as his tongue slowed, carrying me over the edge and keeping me hovering over the ground for so long, a thin sheen of sweat dotted my skin.

"Damn," he whispered as he smacked his lip. "You taste like berries."

His lips closed around my clit and he kissed me, pulling another long aftershock from me.

"That . . . *those* were amazing, but now I need you to fill me up, Savior. Right. Fucking. Now."

His grin turned dark, salacious as his hand cupped my pussy, making me pulse and leak some more.

"Since you asked so nicely."

His words were gravelly, thick with hunger as he stroked his cock, giving me the first real look at the long, hard piece of meat. He looked even thicker than he felt as he slid closer, sliding the tip of his cock through my slick lips.

"Fuck, girl. You're so hot and so fucking tight. Shit!"

I smiled as my body pulsed around him, flooded until the friction was so delightful so all-consuming that the only thing that existed was our bodies, sliding against one another in the never-ending pursuit of pleasure. His hips picked up speed, pounding and thrusting feverishly as though he couldn't get deep enough. It was an intoxicating feeling that set my skin —hell, my soul – on fire.

"Savior, fuck. Don't stop."

He grinned that dark, mischievous grin of his that made his blue eyes look like they had an actual twinkle in them, held my inner thighs wide open and pounded into me until both of us were covered in sweat, panting as we grabbed at each other, desperate to find something concrete to hold on to. Pleasure sending us drifting into an abyss, lost to everything but each other and our pleasure. He was close. I felt the way his cock thickened and hardened inside me and that was all it took for me to slingshot off that ledge once more, completely sated.

Boneless.

Spineless.

Damn near lethargic.

When Savior came, it was long and forceful, barreling out of him so hard, his face twisted in an animalistic pleasure that was so captivating, I couldn't look away.

"Fuck . . . Mandy!"

When his big body collapsed on me, his tongue licking at the tendon between my neck and shoulder, I shivered as aftershocks rocked my overheated body.

"Okay, fine. You've convinced me to let you drive. But only because I am entirely too worn out to do anything."

His deep chuckle was the only response.

***

"Damn Mandy! Who knew you had all that underneath those jeans and tees you wear?"

DELICIOUSLY DAMAGED

Teddy basically catcalled me as I drew closer to where she and Jana sat on the area reserved for the pre-wedding beach barbecue.

I looked down at the silky green halter dress I grabbed because Teddy had insisted it made my eyes pop and would highlight the slope of my neck, because apparently that was something that required highlighting.

"It's just a dress. You both look great."

They were both glowing the luminescent look of women in love and bringing life to the world. I'd seen it plenty, that look pregnant women had. People always talked about the *glow*, but I was convinced it all came from the eyes.

"Thanks," Jana said with a pout, rubbing her swollen bump. "But we look like fatties in fine textiles, especially compared to you. If I didn't like you so much, I'd probably hate you."

I laughed. "Thanks, I think."

"Don't mind her, Mandy. Jana's just upset she's so big she can only get it doggy style now."

I frowned. "That doesn't sound like a problem to me." Hell, I'd always thought it was the best way to have sex because then you didn't have to look your partner in the face and remember it later. Nope. Just the memory of the cock, not the man.

"Yeah well, maybe you don't have a man as sexy and handsome as mine," she said with that dreamy look on her face single women loathed.

"Since I don't have a man at all, that's probably accurate," I said casually.

Besides, I'd never been so smitten with anyone like that. No man had ever made me smile that way or said such cheesy things to me.

"Besides, you have to say that since you're marrying him."

They both laughed at my words, giving me that "wait 'til it happens to you" look.

"Did you really ride here with Savior?"

Both women leaned forward as much as they could, given their considerable baby bumps, eager to hear any gossip.

"I did."

I gave them a quick rundown of his behavior lately. "He beat me at my own game and then gave me three orgasms this morning until I submitted."

"All right!" Jana and Teddy high fived each other like boys in a locker room.

"Settle down, baby mamas, it was just a little harmless sex. Nothing to go nuts over."

"Ha!" Teddy tilted her head back and laughed. "Everyone who believes that, raise your hand."

I raised mine and she smacked it down with more force than a pregnant woman should be allowed to have.

"That's how it was with me and Max and now we're here for our wedding." Jana gazed down at her wedding bling with a loopy smile on her face.

"Yep, me too. Tate and I were fuck buddies only and now look at us." She wore the same goofy look Jana had, which I guessed was love. They both looked happy and that was what mattered.

"Clearly you both were looking for that. I'm clearly not."

I'd spend the next few days enjoying Savior's hard body and the orgasms he gave me but as soon as we got back to Vegas, I'd keep my distance. There was something in the water in Mayhem and in Vegas and I didn't want any part of it.

"Thanks for inviting me, I've never been to California."

"I'm glad you came," Jana insisted with a genuine smile. "You are part of our group now. Of course you're invited. I just hope you know you can call either of us, just to talk or hang out."

I nodded, hearing what they were both saying.

"I haven't had any real friends in a long time," I told them but the truth was I didn't know if I'd ever had any real friends. Krissy was the closest thing to a friend I'd ever had and she was a user. "It'll take some getting used to, but I'll try my best."

They both smiled but soon the men joined us and both Max and Tate whisked their women off, leaving me on my own. Again. The ocean called to me, as it always did. In New York I spent plenty of time just looking out at the Hudson River and if I could swing it, I'd get out to watch the dark blue waters of the Atlantic. The water here was lighter, cold, but not quite as icy.

The air was salty with a hint of the fishiness that gave many of the people in town their livelihood. Seeing the water, so vast and never ending, made me think of impossible things, like who I would've been if I hadn't lost everyone that mattered to me. It was such a foreign thought, I never got further than simple family dinners with Mom, Dad and Ammo.

"Penny for your thoughts." Savior's deep voice startled me but I didn't turn to look at him, I couldn't. I didn't want him to see what was on my mind.

"My thoughts are too dark for pennies, got any drachmas?" I laughed but he didn't, a sure sign he wasn't buying my attempt at levity. Savior grabbed my hand, and we walked along the water, the music from the party growing more distant with every step.

"No drachmas, but I've got a strong stomach."

I was sure he did, considering what he'd probably seen as a solider and then a Reckless Bastard. But I still didn't want to share my dreams with anyone. "What's your real name?"

"Vick."

"Not quite as cool as Savior, but very hot."

I would've guessed something regular like Mike or Nick, but Vick was the name of a man. A big strong man with a manly ass beard.

"I like it."

He smirked. "Thanks."

"So, how'd you get a name like Savior?"

He snorted. "Some stupid shit before basic."

I smiled and looked up at him. "So tell me. Sound's fun."

"Fun? I wouldn't call anything I did in—or before—the service fun." He stopped and looked out at the water. "Okay, so before I enlisted, I wanted to become a priest. I was—"

"—a priest? Seriously? I didn't realize you had that much Jesus in you." I laughed a little. A priest. Vick looked nothing like a priest and acted like one even less.

"If you're gonna tease, then I'll shut up." He faked a pout.

"No! I want to hear the story. Seriously."

"Okay then, don't laugh. Before I'd ever thought about enlisting, I was a church going man. Priesthood was something I aspired to do. Then after 9/11, I enlisted. Thought I could serve my country. You know, be a good American and all. Well, I may have mentioned it in a conversation in boot camp, you know getting to know the other newbies, and every one of those motherfuckers started calling me Savior. As a joke.

Then, when we made it to the sandbox, shit got real. Shit I don't ever want to see or do again. I saved quite a few men out there, but not all. Unfortunately, we had to send a few soldiers home in body bags, but the name stuck." He breathed in and let it out slowly. "So, there ya go."

We walked in silence for a while before he said anything else. "Do you miss New York?"

"Some days I miss it so much I can hardly stand it but this is where my family is so it's where I am. Even if it turns out to be a really bad idea."

"I won't let it," he said confidently, and I didn't bother to correct him, because it would be pointless. "At least not before you've had a chance to make me your favorite dessert."

I laughed. "Yeah and what is my favorite?"

He shrugged and swung our arms between us. "I don't know, but I loved those strawberry orange cookies you sent in one of your care packages. They were fucking delicious."

I laughed, feeling heat blossom at the memory. "Ammo said you guys were like vultures with those cookies. Told me to only send chocolate chip or peanut butter so you didn't lose your minds.

He laughed at the memory too. "Yeah, I think I ate at least half of them."

Savior leaned close, brushing his lips against the shell of my ear as he spoke.

"Speaking of, it's time for me to get turned on watching you lick barbecue sauce from your fingers."

He pulled me back toward the music and the group of bikers celebrating their friends entering into wedded bliss.

His words were so fucking dirty, so wicked that I felt like I was constantly turned on when he was around. Even when he was doing his best to piss me off.

Chapter 10

Savior

I woke up and rolled over expecting to find a couple handfuls of soft, warm woman, instead I was met by a cool, empty bed.

I called out "Mandy?" but I could tell the room was empty. It was too quiet, so I turned over on my back, smiling as I thought about how wild she'd been after dinner last night.

I never knew women could be ravenous like that. I mean sure, they were eager and dirty, some were legit kinky, but most of the time they were just acting. Last night though, had been sweet, unadulterated Mandy.

My cock was getting hard just thinking about the way she'd pushed me down on the bed and sank between my knees, making love to my dick with her mouth. She'd laid those smiling eyes on me, never looking away as she slowly ripped away every stitch of my control. And now she was gone, which I confirmed by walking through the spacious hotel room overlooking the beach. She'd left a note. *Gone surfin'*, it said, which was strange since I was pretty sure she didn't know how to surf.

After a quick shower, I got dressed and went to find the hot little pixie who'd rocked my world. I found her on the beach in the water with some blond model doing time as a surf instructor, though he was doing more smiling and flirting than instructing. I could see it from the shore. Hell, a blind man could see it. The closer I got, the more I wanted to bash the prick's face in.

But this was her vacation, too, so I sat back and watched. Until he reached out to correct her footing and let his hand linger longer than he needed to.

"There you are."

They both jumped and turned to me.

"Savior," she said, a hint of surprise, and then heat as her gaze slid to my chest.

"Kip, this is Savior. A family friend."

I quirked a brow at her and she gave me one right back.

"Don't let me interrupt your lesson."

I kept my voice even and my face blank. Kip backed up a little.

"Actually we're done," he stammered. "I was just, ah, giving Mandy some pointers."

He scraped one hand through his hair while the other began cutting through the water.

"Just remember to tighten your core. I, uhm, see my next client. Enjoy your vacation," he called out, already paddling fast with his back to us.

"Was that necessary?"

I shrugged. "Don't know what you mean."

"No. I won't do this Neanderthal thing, Savior. It's not my jam. It's my least favorite jam, in fact."

"What?"

"I'll make it simple for you. Knock it off."

She was cute when she was trying to be tough.

"I can't help it, not when you look like you do in that."

I pointed at the bathing suit, or the perfect likeness of one, anyway. Calling it 'barely there' would be generous. Not that I was complaining. The blue fabric looked like one long ribbon molded strategically to drive me out of my fucking mind.

"You've seen me in much less than this."

"Yeah, but when I look at you in that, all I can see is myself unraveling it, kissing and nibbling every inch of skin as I uncover it."

I waded into the water, catching up with her so I could reach over and tug on the bow at her hip but she smacked my hand away.

"You didn't think I'd make it easy for drunken frat boys and frisky bikers, did you?"

"A man can hope, can't he?"

DELICIOUSLY DAMAGED

"I never would have pegged you for an optimist."

She squeaked when I pulled her up against me, treading water and unable to resist the urge to run my hands up and down the smooth skin of her thighs.

"I'm surprising even myself these days."

I pressed a kiss to her neck that made her shiver. "But nothing was as surprising as you. Last night."

"Must be the sea air," she said in a muffled voice against my chest.

"Must be," I agreed in a grave voice. "And I thought it was me."

"You may have played a small part," she said with a laugh and pushed away, paddling back towards the beach.

"Who you callin' small, woman?" I said, stroking after her.

"Don't worry, Savior, you were more than adequate." She giggled as she widened the gap between us.

But I was determined to paddle faster. "You can't run far enough from that, sweetheart!"

"I have excellent upper body strength. I'm a pastry chef!"

My body flamed at the reminder of her strong arms and hands. "I'm bigger."

"Again with the size?" She couldn't hold in her laughter after that, making it easy to catch up with her. "You're a big guy, Savior."

I snorted. "Yeah, thanks. But I know you remember exactly how big I am."

Her cheeks flamed red, nostrils flared.

"I do. Sometimes I swear I can still feel you inside me."

How was I not supposed to tip her board over and take her, hard and fast in the ocean, when she said shit like that to me?

"What time is your spa stuff with the girls?"

Her eyes widened and I knew any plans I'd been making with Mandy and my cock would have to wait.

"Shit, I forgot. What time is it?" She didn't wait for answer, just grabbed my wrist, gasping when my knuckles brushed against one hard titty. "I have to go."

"You sure?" I brushed a hand across the soft skin of her belly, reveling in the way she jumped at my touch. The way I affected her.

"Unfortunately, I am."

"I hate that, but later you're mine." She nodded and brushed my lips against hers, soft and tender. Anything more than that and I'd say fuck both our schedules and carry her back up to the room. We'd reached the beach and she lifted the board out of the water like it was a feather.

"There's a bridesmaid robe for you on the bed."

She laughed. "I have no response to that. See you later."

"Later," I said too quiet for her to hear, but it didn't matter because my focus was on her ass and the sway of her hips as she walked away. A little extra swing just for me.

***

"Man you have been moping all day! That cute little fairy got her hooks into you deep."

Lasso laughed and clapped my back too damn hard as he sat beside me at the table on the beach. Tonight was the rehearsal dinner, but I didn't get it. People have been getting married since religion was invented and they didn't need a practice day for it. As far as I was concerned, though, all the free food and booze was good enough reason to party.

"I'm not moping, asshole. I'm pensive."

"Oh, that's a ten-dollar word. Jag, get me a twenty!"

"Yeah, real funny, Lasso." I punched his shoulder, making him groan.

DELICIOUSLY DAMAGED

"So, if you're not thinking about that sexy little baker, what's on your mind?"

Shit, like I could tell him I couldn't stop thinking about Mandy. I couldn't. I wouldn't. It was just the sex that had me going a little crazy. "Just life, brother."

He barked out a laugh. "If that's what you need to tell yourself, man. But I saw you two earlier in the water. You looked real cozy to me. Like those two over there," he said, pointing to a young couple who were sucking each other's faces right on the beach for everyone to watch. "There's no harm in wanting a woman, especially a fine one like that."

"She's Ammo's sister."

Which was, honestly, only part of the problem. The bigger problem was, well. . .I didn't do serious—or commitment. Women started looking for it right away and I wasn't the guy. And being Ammo's sister, Mandy deserved it all.

"And you were his best friend. There's no other man on the planet he'd trust with his baby sister. No matter what that man thinks of himself."

I had to laugh at his armchair psych words.

"Yeah, thanks man. But we both know I don't do all this," I told him, pointing at the decorations that served as a dedication to love and commitment, *lifelong* commitment. There were hearts and flowers, with a bunch of baby-sized foods on the menu to celebrate the new life they would soon bring into the world. This was a reminder that I wasn't cut out for this life.

"All I know is that you *say* you don't do it. But I also know that Max was too fucked up to even consider fucking the same chick twice less than two years ago and here we are, in San Diego, for his wedding. Hell, Golden Boy was locked up, wrongfully imprisoned for years, man. If that doesn't fuck with your ability to trust . . ." he trailed off with a long low whistle. "Well, he'll be marching down the aisle soon too."

DELICIOUSLY DAMAGED

All of that was true, damn him, but irrelevant. "They aren't me."

I didn't have shit to offer any woman, never mind one like Mandy. She'd already lost too much to end up with a guy born to a crack whore who had no problems abandoning her son for some asshole with a little cash in his pocket, and a drunk who'd never been curious about the kid he sired. One who lied and stole with ease. Sure, I'd done it just to survive, but in the end, none of that mattered.

"Whatever you say." He stood and smacked my back again, this time with a purposeful harshness I couldn't ignore. "Then I guess you won't mind if I ask her for a dance."

His gaze lifted toward the open doors of the hotel restaurant where Mandy stood, looking like a pixie goddess in her deep pink dress that draped over her curves with expert precision. It was silk or some other shiny fabric and it made my hands twitch to touch her.

"I damn well do mind."

I put a hand to his chest to stop his path toward Mandy and ignored Lasso's deep chuckle. "Find your own goddamn woman."

"I already have," he said, his gaze drifting toward a leggy redhead holding a silver tray filled with champagne glasses. "See you in a bit."

"Don't count on it," I told him, my legs already carrying me to Mandy as she nervously smoothed her short hair.

"Mandy, damn you look like a dirty dream I had recently."

Her soft laugh carried on the ocean breeze. "Yeah? Thanks. Who knew you looked so good without a stitch of denim or leather in sight?"

Her gaze was hot and hungry as she took me in, the suit we'd all slipped into at Jana's insistence.

She'd laid down the law. "I don't care that you're bikers, I love my biker man. But you will damn well not look like bikers for my wedding."

DELICIOUSLY DAMAGED

All of us had obeyed, more terrified of the tiny blonde than any threats we'd ever faced fighting for Uncle Sam.

"You should see me without any denim or leather on. At all."

"I have, and I have to say, I prefer you without any of it." She licked her lips seductively, her eyes flicked up and down the length of my body as she took in every detail.

"Just say the word, babe."

Her cheeks turned a delicious shade of pink as she bit down on her bottom lip.

"I have so many words to say, Savior. But I think they're waiting for us," she said, gesturing to where Teddy stood in the center of a large group waving frantically at them.

"Come on."

She grabbed my hand and pulled me along, stopping to kick off her heels, so sharp and pointy, I knew I'd ask her to put them back on for me later.

It took a total of five fucking minutes to get through the actual rehearsal for tomorrow's wedding, Teddy and Golden Boy walked down the makeshift sandy aisle together, and then Mandy and Cross, followed by several other Reckless Bastards that Max had insisted stand up with him on this important day, me included. They pretended to go through the vows, but Mandy and Cross did it in place of the happy couple, some shit about bad luck. I figured if we were here for the wedding, it was too late to worry about something jinxing the relationship.

"And now, we eat!" Teddy clapped her hands to herd everyone toward the long table set up just for us, right on the beach.

I tried to wait for Mandy, eager to get my hands on her and that silky dress under the table, but the distance between us seemed to grow. Literally, every fucking time I looked up, there were more Reckless Bastards, more beachcombers between us.

"I'm starved," I said.

"Me too," Lasso groaned. "But Sierra is working until eleven, so I guess I'll just eat the food until then."

I laughed. "You have problems, man. Serious fucking problems."

Lasso joined in. "You have no idea, brother."

He was right. All I knew was that he had family back in Texas that he never talked about or talked to. Or went to visit. "Then I guess you're my date for the evening."

"No offense, bro, but I'd rather stare at Mandy's face while I eat. Yo, Mandy!"

She turned at Lasso's loud twang, smiling in confusion at his wide grin. She spotted me and her grin brightened, waved as she carefully made her way to our table. "Hey guys, did you save me a seat?"

"Here, take mine," Lasso offered with his most chivalrous smile, Texas charm a mile wide and twice as deep. "He was miserable without you, sweetheart."

"Yeah?" She flashed a teasing grin my way. "Then I'll make sure to eat with my hands, remind him of what a lousy dinner companion I am."

Lasso tossed his head back and laughed. "I really like her, Savior. Keep her or I'm stealing her."

"I am a woman, not a piece of property, thank you very much!" She crossed her arms, doing her best to look offended. "Besides, I'd never let myself get stolen by a guy named after a rope."

He laughed again, shaking his head as he walked away. "I think Lasso likes you."

Her smile was sweet. "He's a decent guy. Too much charm, but he seems nice enough. And I'm an expert at spotting the not so nice ones."

I knew there was more there, but tonight I didn't want to hear it. Tonight, I wanted to enjoy the beach and the food, the booze and Mandy. "Yeah, he's good people."

"You all seem to be," she said with a sigh. "You know, when I was kid, I resented the hell out of you fuckers. I imagined the absolute worst because it made it easier to hate you than own up to the fact that my brother, my hero, preferred you all to me."

"Mandy, it wasn't like that."

"I know," she said on a sigh. "With age and hindsight, came wisdom. The resentment went away. I'm happy he had a family again."

Damn, this girl killed me. She fucking gutted me and . . . I didn't know how the fuck to feel about that. Women didn't get to me, not outside the bedroom. They could make me holler, shake and come, but they didn't *get* to me.

"You have that now."

"No, I don't. But that's okay, you know. I've learned to live without it and it's not so bad."

"You don't want a tribe of your own?"

She had to. Even the most fucked up of the Reckless Bastards had survived because of us. We kept our shit together, our noses mostly clean because of the club. The brotherhood. Because we knew there were other people relying on us.

"I don't know. I haven't had one since I was a little girl so I haven't given it much thought. I do well on my own." She seemed to believe her words but I knew it was because she didn't know the comfort of having a tribe, a family.

And I also knew why I couldn't get her out of my mind. Fucking Ammo, meddling bastard that he was. Found a way to give his kid sister the family he'd always wanted for her.

"For now, we should agree to disagree."

Her brow arched. "Sounds like you plan to try and change my mind."

I shrugged. "I can be very persuasive when I have to be. Or even better, when I want to be."

"Yes, but is your meat this juicy?" She stabbed a thick slice of steak from the platter and bit into it with the most sinful moan.

DELICIOUSLY DAMAGED

    Never in my life had I found myself so jealous of a piece of fucking steak.

Chapter 11

Mandy

The sounds of the rehearsal dinner in full party mode grew distant as I walked further up the beach. The sun had set hours ago, the dark sky and the water could meet in secret now and I couldn't look away. I'd always loved the ocean, and tonight with the stars twinkling beautifully, it was magnificent and soothing.

Tonight though, everything made me think of Ammo. Probably because this was the first time I'd hung out with a big group of people that didn't include my classmates or just a crowded bar. These guys, they were a family. Unconventional, sure, but undoubtedly family. They had each other's back through all kinds of shit and, despite what I'd told Savior, I did envy it. It wasn't something I'd pictured for myself, but to know you have that kind of support, I did miss having that. Or maybe I missed the memories of it. But Ammo, he'd had this, and that meant a lot to me, to know that we both didn't walk alone all this time.

Still, it was so unfair. It should be Ammo getting married this weekend with a kid on the way, maybe a few nieces and nephews already that I would have spoiled.

"Hey, you okay?" Savior's voice pulled me from my thoughts, his hand on my shoulder startled, then settled me.

"I'm as good as I ever am, Savior. Are you enjoying yourself?"

He laughed.

"More than I thought I would. They do know how to put on a party."

His voice was warm, full of affection. One arm hooked around my waist and pulled me close.

"I'm happy for them."

"Me too," I told him quietly.

"I miss him too."

His whispered words made me shiver, his warm beer-sweetened breath fanned across my neck. "Days like this, so much I can hardly stand it."

"I've never been to a wedding or a wedding celebration before, but I can admit that Ammo has been on my mind a lot today."

More since I came back to Vegas than he had in the months before I'd returned home.

"Never? I figured as a pastry chef you'd been to plenty."

"The chef I apprenticed with didn't do weddings unless they were megastars or royals. Mostly we did exclusive parties for the one percent, or the rich and powerful who visited the restaurant."

He fell into step beside me and we kept walking along the water.

He whistled. "Sounds fancy."

"Hardly," I snorted. "But it's nice to cook for people who appreciate really good food."

"We all like good food."

"Maybe, but some appreciate better food."

He snorted his disbelief but I didn't need to brag.

"When we're back in Mayhem," I said, "bring over two burgers from your favorite place in town, we'll do a taste test."

"You'll cook naked?"

I laughed. "You have a one-track mind, Savior."

"Well if my cock wasn't so lonely this morning," he pulled me close again, pressing my back against the cool rock structure that formed a small cove. "Maybe my mind would have more tracks to travel."

"Or maybe you're just a sex addict, ah!" I groaned when he slid one warm hand up my leg to my inner thigh and brushed his fingers over my pussy. "Shit."

"That sounded like a yes," he groaned, sliding my panties to the side as one finger, then two slipped inside. "But I'm willing to work for it."

DELICIOUSLY DAMAGED

His mouth crashed down onto mine and I swear, in less than a minute his mouth and his fingers had my whole body shaking with intensity. His fingers plunged deep and fast, this thumb creating dangerous circles on my clit.

"Savior," I moaned in his ear as his lips went to my neck, skating across sensitive flesh, now cooled by the ocean breeze. "Fuck, yeah."

I hung on to him as my orgasm washed over me, so fast I should've been ashamed. I wasn't. At all. He had the ability to make me explode with just a touch, and he wielded that power with expert precision.

"Shit," I hissed, trembling inside and out.

"You already said that." His deep chuckle gave me a shudder of aftershocks that had Savior pulling me closer, kissing a line from my neck to my shoulders. "But it didn't sound like a yes."

"What am I saying yes to, again?"

He laughed and kissed me, right there under the moonlight, kissed me until my legs shook and I had no choice but to hang on to him, or drift away forever.

"Does it matter? Just say yes, sweet Mandy."

I didn't know what I was saying yes to, but with his lips and hands all over my body, the gentle kiss of the salty sea air, it didn't matter all that much. He could have stripped me bare right there on the beach, took me hard and fast while the partiers looked on, and I would have let him. I pulled back with a smile, licking my lips as I said the word we both wanted to hear.

"Yes."

***

There was a tickle behind my knee, making it hard for me to sneak in the last hour of sleep before I had to get ready for the morning. Today Jana and Max were getting married, and I was going to help them start their marriage on the right foot. It was kind of ironic, the girl with no family being such a big part of helping two people become one. It was a unique experience and one I was both excited and honored to share with my new friends.

That tickle persisted, this time moving up my leg until I felt the tickle of a beard and purred. "Good morning."

"It is now. Christ, woman, I thought I was gonna have to start jumping on the bed to wake you."

Savior frowned, his blue eyes looked like crushed sapphires in the morning sun, and I just laughed.

"Maybe if you were a little more insistent, I would have woken up with a smile."

I giggled when he growled and nibbled on the inside of my thigh. Me, Mandy Sutton, found herself giggling. With a sexy, bearded biker wearing a determined glint.

"I can do insistent," he said, using his shoulders to push my thighs apart. His hands were warm just like the rest of him, his breath whispered against my core, cool against the slickness. He spread me apart, blowing gently until I moaned.

"Watch."

"Yeah, okay," I panted. He was so close to where I wanted him, where I craved him, but not close enough, dammit.

"Mandy." His voice, deep and commanding, held me captive. "Watch. Don't look away."

Shit, how could I look away when he wore that look. I didn't want to miss one fucking second of this show. And I didn't. From the moment his tongue lapped at my clit, slid deep into my body, I couldn't tear my gaze from him. Eyes closed, pink tongue darting in and out, like a dance where he figured out which steps drove me out of my mind the fastest.

"Savior," I moaned, arching my back.

He smiled and his gaze held mine, but his mouth never stopped torturing me. Loving me. Teasing me. Everything he did, included exaggerated motions so I could see explicitly what he was doing to me. He fucked me with his tongue, teased my clit with his teeth, his tongue, his whole mouth. Sucked me in and tugged hard until lightning flew out of my pores, his name flew from my mouth like a prayer. Or a curse. I held his head, watching him as I ground against his face, his slick smile driving me towards another orgasm. He pulled back.

"Number two's on me." He stood and reached for my ankle, pulling me to the edge of the bed. "Literally."

I reached out to him, wrapping my hand around his long, thick cock, licking the bead of liquid perched at the tip. He really was beautifully built, his cock was long and thick, the head a perfect mushroom that slid against every one of my nerve endings when he plunged deep inside me. It was damn near perfect as far as I was concerned.

"Mandy," he grunted, tugging on my hair and making me moan. "You're a fucking dirty girl, aren't you?"

He smacked my ass on the last word, punctuating his question with a smack.

"Oh!" I squeaked at the initial burst of pain but the pain hadn't left when the pleasure came, fanning out over the area and making my pussy pulse. He did it again on the other side and I wasn't surprised by my reaction this time. "Maybe I am."

He laughed, rubbing soothing circles over the places where he'd spanked me.

"You definitely are," he said with absolute certainty as his cock head nudged my opening from behind, sank deep, long and slow. "Fuck, Mandy. Always so fucking wet for me."

"She's hungry for her favorite meat," I told him, drawing a hearty laugh from him that was in stark contrast to the heat of the moment.

"She won't go hungry on my watch," he said, holding my hips so he could slide as deep as he wanted. "Fuck, Mandy," he grunted as he pulled out and thrust deep, again and again, his breaths coming in fast and shallow.

DELICIOUSLY DAMAGED

It was so good. Too good. The kind of good that made you shout outrageous things in the throes of passion, the kind of good that could make you forget everything else in your life.

"More, Savior. More! Yes!"

A primal grunt ripped from his mouth, his knee swept mine until the whole front of my body was flat on the bed, his body pasted against my back. From this position, I was defenseless. I could do nothing but accept the pleasure he laid on me. The sharp, passionate bites on my shoulder and neck, the hard way he gripped my hips as he pounded into me.

"Fuck my cock, baby, this pussy is mine!"

My body shivered at his words, at the way he grabbed my ass and spread my cheeks, sinking deeper into me. So deep I couldn't tell if we were still two people, and that was dangerous thinking this time of morning. On a wedding day. With a guy like him. I pushed that thought away, because he grabbed my wrists in one of his hands, holding them above my head as he held me in place with the other, pounding into me for all he was worth. So hard, so deep that the sound of our slick skin smacking together blended with our moans for an intense rhythm that pulsed through my whole body.

"Savior," I warned.

"Let go Mandy. I got you."

So I did. He sank his teeth into that spot at the crook of my neck, pounding so hard and fast into me that my orgasm spilled out of me like a bucket overflowing with water.

"Oh, god! Vick, yes, fuck yes!"

And then I was lost to the pleasurable energy, the passion that flowed out of me like warm honey while Savior continued to drive into me, in search of his own pleasure.

"You're so fucking beautiful when you come."

"I'm face down," I told him, squeezing my inner muscles until he groaned.

"Yeah but the way your shoulders and neck turn pink just before that orgasm explodes out of you, makes me harder every time I see it."

He sat up, leaving my back cool and damp as he pulled my hips up so my ass was exposed to him.

"I can't get enough of you," he growled, sliding back into me on a long, hard thrust.

"Fuck, yes," I moaned. "No one is asking you to."

He held my hips with both hands, pounding so deep that my arms shook. I arched my back and he sank into me, shouting as his orgasm surprised him, barreled out of him and right into me.

"Mandy." He said nothing else, just my name, over and over.

I liked that.

I liked it more than I should.

"Too bad there's a wedding in a few hours," I finally said when I could breathe normally.

"Or, it's a good thing we need to be extra clean on this very special day. We'll need a long, hot shower," he grinned.

"And we should probably do it together, right? Better for the environment that way."

"Anything to help out Mother Earth," he grinned again, pulling me to my feet.

"You, Savior, are a true conservationist," I joked with him, but this fun, warm feeling felt a hell of a lot like trouble to me. The kind of messy trouble that left a girl with runny mascara and no faith in herself. The kind of messy I did my best to avoid.

I ignored the warmth and the affection, focusing instead on the heat and intensity. The hunger that was always there between us.

Chapter 12

Savior

Some people were suckers at weddings. They got all sappy and misty-eyed as the bride walked down the aisle, love shining in her eyes as she made her way to the man who could see nothing but her. Here, among battle scarred bikers and chicks with more than their fair share of issues, the romantics stood out. Surprisingly, Mandy wasn't one of them. She wore a pretty smile and she seemed genuinely happy for them, but not longing for what they had.

I wasn't ashamed to admit that I felt some relief at that. Having the girl you're sleeping with getting moon-eyed and sappy at a wedding wasn't exactly the path toward keeping shit uncomplicated. Despite my worries, I could appreciate the beautiful simplicity of the wedding. Jana's pregnant belly couldn't be contained by the gauzy white dress she wore, molding over the kid we'd all meet as soon as the wind blew. She couldn't stop smiling, tears shining in her eyes as she and Max held hands and promised to love each other forever and ever. I wasn't all that sure about forever, to be honest, but if anyone had a shot — it was Max and Jana.

We'd nearly lost Max to PTSD and if not for Jana, we probably would have. Her and those damn painting classes had saved our boy, so not only was she one of us, Jana was the fucking *best* of us. And when they shared their first kiss as man and wife, even a cynical fucker like me felt like the world had gotten something right.

The ceremony was beautiful, at least according to Teddy who had run everything with the skill of a five-star general, and Jana, who couldn't stop gushing as we all stood, posing for pictures. I wondered how many damn photos one couple needed as the photographer rotated the bride and groom, the best man, Golden Boy and Maid of Honor, Teddy, and then the other bridesmaid, Mandy, along with me, Cross, Lasso and Jag. So many fucking pictures.

DELICIOUSLY DAMAGED

"Thank fuck," I groaned when the photographer hurried off to get some scenic shots.

Max chuckled and wrapped his arms around his wife. "Sorry babe, but Savior is right. I don't think our place is big enough for all the photos he took."

"All right, shut up," she said with a laugh, waving her hands to stop all the jokes about the wedding photos. "It's over now and you all survived. Big babies."

She went down the line, hugged each of the Reckless Bastards who had stood up with her and Max today.

"Thank you guys. You all look so handsome today, I'm glad I got tons of proof."

She laughed at our shocked faces, squealing when Golden Boy picked her up off the ground, smacking a kiss to her cheek. "Stop that Tate, before this baby drops right out of me."

With a collective groan, her words drove the men away. Mandy chose that moment to join Jana and

Teddy. "Hey wifey, let's get you off your feet for a few minutes."

Jana laughed, cheeks pink with embarrassment but eyes alight with gratitude for Mandy's thoughtfulness. "Thank, Mandy. I probably would have run myself ragged."

"Somehow I don't think the baby biker would have allowed it. One of my instructors got pregnant and she would get so tired during night classes she would fall asleep standing up, leaning on the wall. Once she fell asleep while making a ganache."

"She did not!" Jana looked horrified.

"She did, whisk in her hand and everything."

"Now I don't feel so bad," Jana said, letting Mandy drag her off in search of a place to sit.

"You like her." Teddy stood beside me, arms crossed on top of her barely showing belly. "We like her too, but she's skittish. More than I was when I met Jana. Try not to fuck it up."

DELICIOUSLY DAMAGED

"Thanks for the vote of confidence, but there's nothing to fuck up. We're friends. Nothing more."

"Hmph, well then." She laid a sympathetic hand on my shoulder; at least I chose to see it that way, even after I caught a glimpse of pity in her eyes. "Too bad." She walked away, shaking her head.

It wasn't too bad. It was just fine. Mandy and I were just having fun, scratching an itch, that was all. She had no hopes where I was concerned, and I was too fucked up for anyone to lay any hope on me. I came from a shit family whose shittiness went back generations. You name it and we had it. Junkies, thieves, whores, numbers runners, bootleggers, hit men, henchmen, kingpins, outlaws and murderers. It was a real impressive bloodline that left no hope of normal, no hope of permanent happiness with white picket fences and babies. I couldn't do that to another person, and I certainly wouldn't send more of us out into this fucking world.

Nope. No, thank you. Not gonna fucking happen.

By the time the reception officially started, the sun had begun to set and we were all ready to party. I had a drink in my hand, half watching as Max spun his pregnant wife on the makeshift dance floor on the beach, while the rest of me scanned the beach for Mandy.

"Looking for someone?"

I smiled as Mandy circled my body, stopping right in front of me.

"Yeah, a hot little blonde in a pink low-cut dress. You seen her?"

The way her mouth curled, all slow and sultry like it was a mini seduction, made my pants grow tighter. "First of all, it's cerise *not* pink. Secondly, I thought I saw her pigging out by the crab cakes."

"There are crab cakes?"

She laughed. "Yeah. You know, you clean up nice, Savior."

"Yeah, well, don't get used to it."

DELICIOUSLY DAMAGED

She shrugged and moved beside me, looking out at the lapping waves. "I'm not invested in your wardrobe either way."

Well, damn. "How'd you like your first wedding?"

"It was . . . nice. I mean I know Jana some, and Max seems like a decent guy, so I'm happy for them, but I just don't get it." Her nose wrinkled adorably. "Jana loved it though and that's what matters."

"Now, we party."

She grinned mischievously, tapping her chin. "In that case, I think I'll go get myself a drink." She turned but I grabbed her hand.

"I'll come with you."

"You usually do," she said with a husky laugh. I stood behind her as she pressed up against the bar. "I'll have a dirty martini, chilled," she smiled at the young bartender, arching her back so it brushed up against my cock.

"And a whiskey, neat." I practically growled the words, grabbing Mandy's hips to keep her still. "You're playing with fire."

She looked up at me over her shoulder, biting on that lush bottom lip. "What?"

I pressed my hips into her, drawing a gasp from her. "That."

"Savior, there you are!" *Fuck.* Teddy's voice cut through the thick haze of desire that surrounded us. "Come on and dance with Jana so we can cut the photographer loose."

I took a step back, smiling softly at the little disappointed moan Mandy let out.

"Not to be a smartass, but isn't it kind of hard to take photos of people when they're moving?"

Teddy laughed and pulled me away from the bar toward the dance floor.

"You would think, but Aris said it could be done and Jana wants him to try. The good news is that while you and Mandy were dry humping at the bar, everyone else has already had their turn."

I glared at her. "We weren't dry humping."

"Right. Because you're friends and nothing more?"

I nodded.

"Good luck with that. While you dance with the bride, I'm going to go find my former *friend and nothing more*, who I will be marrying as soon as we decide on a date."

"You're a real pain. It's a good thing you're pretty."

She rolled her eyes. "Tough, too, buster. I'm only letting you get away with that because Mandy might need your other parts later."

I barked out a laugh. "You are nothing but trouble, Red."

"And, baby," she said with a groan as she rubbed her belly.

"All right, I'm going." I didn't get all the little wedding traditions but dancing with a pretty lady, even one that belonged to a fellow brother, was never a hardship.

Even if what I really wanted was to wrap my arms around another pretty lady, one with a short little pixie cut that made my hands itch to run through her soft, silky hair.

Chapter 13

Mandy

"I hope you don't think this means a goddamn thing, little girl. You may be hot shit *now* but come talk to me in twenty years."

Landry was on a roll, anger spitting from his pores over the less than stellar review he'd gotten while I was away.

"I've seen plenty of chefs like you come and go, then *poof*, obscurity."

Spit flew out of his mouth and, unlike the other kitchen workers, I dodged that shit. The man had a compulsion about eating raw onions. No, thanks.

The wedding was a few weeks ago, and I had my head down since I returned to work. But my stoicism this morning only stoked his anger.

"You are the only one competing, Landry. I'm just working, nothing more." Working him was exhausting and I didn't feel like I'd gained much more than a headache. In fact, I was starting to think that leaving wouldn't be the worst thing in the world.

"Just shut up and get back to work!" Arms crossed, he leaned forward with a scowl on his face but my gaze just focused on the one drop of sweat sliding down his forehead and around one of the red bulbous nostrils of his nose.

"There's a cheesecake order for the Casino Owner's Association luncheon being held here tomorrow and it sure as shit won't bake itself! Got it?"

I nodded, not bothering to tell him that the cake was already done. That while he was blustering about the crepes he'd butchered this morning and the cookies that had crumbled during plating, I'd already baked it and had it cooling on a rack.

Because unlike him, I was a fucking professional. I planned to come in early tomorrow to finish the glaze and decorating, but again, not anything he needed to know. Luckily with his tirade over, I could get back to work and pretend I was somewhere else. Like the amazing chefs I'd worked with pretty much everywhere else, men and women who loved to teach, who got off on making sure they sent out well-trained chefs who might end up outshining them.

I spent the last few hours of my shift rolling out dough, piping, glazing and creaming. All the shit work Landry heaped my way that was usually left up to interns and preppers. All day. All week, really. I did it all, without complaint. Oh, I told him off in my mind. Imagined the worst things in the world happening to him, like my personal favorite, him getting caught in the industrial mixer as the paddle sliced through him. But I said nothing, just to piss him off.

I was so close to freedom when Landry stopped me again as I was heading out for the day. "I'm watching you, girl. I won't let you come in here and steal my job. Better chefs, hell better men *and* women than you have tried, failed and lived to fucking regret it."

I stared at him, spittle gathered on the rim of his bottom lip, the corner of his mouth and it struck me as funny. Hilarious, in fact. And I laughed. I knew I should have controlled it, and I would have if I could, but sometimes I couldn't do shit about a laugh but let it happen. "I'm sorry," I said but it was undercut by another fit of laughter.

"Laugh it up, Mandy."

My eyes rolled so hard I'd thought I'd go blind for a minute. "Do what you have to do Landry. I'm not trying to steal your job, and that's the truth. I came here thinking I could learn from you and then move on. But maybe I should just skip to the part where I move on."

I wasn't ready to quit just yet, but then again, fate had never left many decisions up to me anyway.

Landry just glared down at me. I shrugged and pushed the door open, waiting for him to speak.

He said nothing, so I left him with, "Let me know."

I walked out feeling a little better, well, also kind of numb, but mostly better, because, fuck him.

When I got home, two pregnant women waited for me.

DELICIOUSLY DAMAGED

The tall redhead announced, "We're going out to eat."

Teddy leaned against the front hood, looking like a leggy preggo fantasy centerfold. Jana was smarter, getting out of the blistering heat and relaxing inside the car with the air blowing on her.

I blinked. "Okay. Congratulations?"

"Everybody's a comedian," Teddy groaned and pushed off the car. "We're pregnant, we're hungry and you probably haven't eaten all day. Get in."

"Sorry but I just spent all day sweating balls in a hot kitchen. If you want me to go anywhere, I need a shower."

I glared until she rolled her eyes. "We'll wait here. Jana's too pregnant for stairs."

I laughed, shaking my head. I envied the friendship they had. They'd known each other for longer than I knew anyone other than my family. I'd worked so I wouldn't have to have roommates, but New York prices made that nothing but a pipe dream. I lived with people that I never knew, never made an effort to get to know beyond basic hanging out if our days off happened to coincide.

It took me no time to shower and change into jeans and a tank top, then get out there before the neighbors thought I was keeping pregnant women locked in a car. "Okay, want me to drive?"

Teddy glared. "You sayin' I'm too fat to drive, pixie? Are ya?"

"Seriously? No, I'm saying I'm worried you might fall asleep at the wheel."

"Oh. Don't worry about that, I just woke up from a nap." She flashed a devilish grin as she backed out of the parking space and drove too fast to an upscale burger joint I hadn't eaten at yet.

"How are you a chef and you haven't tried this place yet," Teddy asked in disbelief as soon as we were seated.

I shrugged. "I haven't had the time. Or the energy."

DELICIOUSLY DAMAGED

"That's a shame, these burgers are the bomb."

Jana laughed, smacking the table, her eyes wide with shock. "Did you just say 'da bomb'?"

"I did."

"The nineties called, they want their slang back."

Teddy rolled her eyes. "It's called retro, bitch. I'm about to be a mom, I'm embracing old school."

I laughed at their banter. It was sharp and sarcastic, but it was filled with a deep affection that resonated with every word. I listened for a long time as Jana talked about their honeymoon, they talked about pregnancy symptoms, too much in my opinion, but the salad starters were delicious.

"And what about you and Savior?" Jana asked. "What's going on there?"

"Not a damn thing," I told them honestly. "I haven't seen him since he dropped me off after the wedding."

That didn't disappoint me, but it also didn't surprise me either.

"How can that be?" Teddy sat up, full of outrage on my behalf. "I saw you two sneak off, probably to the same supply closet I dragged Tate to later. Much later."

"You did. We did. And it was hot, really fucking hot."

But it had also been incredibly intense, so hot and intense, so *something* I couldn't name but I felt it down to my soul. It was too much, and it shook Savior even more. He'd pretty much shut down after that. Except when he reached for me in the night. Twice.

"But?" Jana was impatient, stabbing at her salad with more force than the arugula required.

"But what?"

I didn't know what to say. That wasn't true. I wasn't sure *how* to say it to them. I kept my own secrets. I was my own advisor. But looking around the table, I knew if I wanted this friendship, I had to start somewhere.

"It's easier if we don't have to guess," Teddy offered with no sympathy.

"Teddy," Jana admonished her with a frown, still stabbing hungrily at her salad.

Teddy raised her shoulders as if she shouldn't have to explain. "I'm just saying. This is what we do, talk. So, open up."

She was right. So, painful as it was, I dipped my toe into this river called friendship and began. "It was intense, too intense. For both of us. Afterwards things got weird." A small sigh escaped, as though I was breathless from sharing. The wading had turned into a deep dive into my emotions.

Two heads shook in unison. "Men," Jana said, that one word dripping with disgust.

"Idiots," Teddy added, equally upset. On my behalf.

"Thanks girls, but really, it's not a big deal. I wasn't expecting anything."

"Yeah, well maybe you should." Teddy stared at me, her gaze serious.

"Oh please!" Jana doubled over the table with laughter, pushing aside her now empty salad bowl. "Teddy likes to forget that she was all fuck 'em and dump 'em before Tate. Hell, even he was just some quick, convenient booty. Before they fell in loo-oove," she sang, ending the note with a gag.

"How am I friends with such a bitch?" Teddy pondered out loud.

I laughed again. "You're both nuts, that's what I've learned today."

"And that men — our men — would rather face bullets than emotions," Jana added with authority.

"Your men," I corrected. "I don't have a man." The server arrived with our burgers, cleared the salad plates and we all dug in, eating quietly for a few minutes. Well, I kept plowing through my slider sampler while they paused politely. To grill me.

DELICIOUSLY DAMAGED

"You know, Mandy, just because neither of you realize it, doesn't mean he isn't yours." Jana gave words of wisdom around a bite of chili cheeseburger.

Her words nearly ruined my three bites of blue cheese and bacon slider. Nearly. "Or maybe it was just a few hot romps? That's okay with me. I don't do connections."

Teddy snorted. "We've noticed."

I rolled my eyes and Jana jumped in. "It's not a criticism, we were the same way. *Are* the same way. We met at a support group for survivors, not college like most people. We were both too fucked up for that. Well, I was anyway."

Teddy wiped the corners of her mouth with her napkin and then gave a piece of her story. "I wasn't, but being a model meant I could fake it with the best of them," she said with a teasing wink. "But we learned to do it because handling shit on your own is the worst."

I shrugged, as if they were speaking a foreign language. "It's what I know."

Jana smiled. "Then we'll teach you," she said gently. "And don't think you can get out of it," she added with an attempt at a mean scowl.

"You don't scare me, little girl." I pointed at her face, shocking her.

"Little? You have what, half an inch on me?"

Teddy snorted. "Ask a man, they'll tell you half an inch can make a big difference." And just like that, the tension at the table burst as we all laughed. And ate. And laughed some more.

It was a good day.

A damn good day.

***

"Mandy, wait up!"

I recognized Krissy's voice instantly and I didn't wait. I sped up. Fuck her. I didn't have time for her bullshit. Not today. Not when I hadn't decided what I would do about my Krissy problem.

"Mandy!"

Her heeled boots sounded on the concrete, her heavy breaths coming closer.

"What the fuck?" she demanded.

"Take a hint," I tossed back at her as I kept walking.

She grabbed my shoulder and I jerked away, pulling my arm back.

"Jeez, someone's jumpy."

"Don't you fucking touch me girl," I warned, facing her now so she could see the fire in my eyes.

"Fine, just slow down or stop for fuck's sake!"

I stopped and glared at her while she explained.

"Look, I borrowed some money from Roadkill MC a while back and then shit went bad and I couldn't pay."

She dragged a shaky hand through her hair, proof it wasn't just gambling getting her into trouble these days.

"You made counting look easy, but it's not. The more decks they added, the worse I did."

She pulled out a cigarette and lit it to stop her shaky hands. The hole she'd dug was impossible to pay back without a little luck. A hell of a lot of luck.

"I'm sure you could work it off somehow."

Her brittle, bitter laugh almost made me cave, but I knew I hadn't heard the punch line. I just kept listening.

"They'd have me whoring myself out or shoving drugs up my cunt, no thanks. Two hundred grand is a lot of cocks to suck."

And there it was. That mercenary, selfish behavior that I hadn't been able to recognize as a needy teenager, but now I saw that shit clear as day.

"So it's okay for me to risk everything when, by my count, you'll take all the earnings just to pay back your bikers? Same old Krissy."

Her head darted around like she was high on something. I knew it was fear. "Come on, Mandy. This is my only shot."

She sucked on the cigarette like she wished it *was* something harder, her eyes hard and wild.

"Then you should be practicing instead of bothering me." I dug my hand into my purse, because that wild look in her eyes got a little too twitchy for my liking.

She was doing that dancing, pleading thing like she needed a fix. "Please, Mandy. Just do this for me. We used to be friends once."

I laughed. "And back then I was too stupid to realize that I took all the risk and you reaped half the benefits. Now you want it all. As tempting as that sounds, I'll pass."

People didn't change and I hated myself for having even one fucking flicker of hope that she was someone different. Someone better. My feet couldn't carry me away from her fast enough.

She called after me, "Mandy, I already told them you'd help. These aren't guys you say no to."

I called back, "You shouldn't have done that," and sped up toward my car. I knew this probably meant I was in this shit knee-deep now, but no matter what I did, I would not help her or those fuckers.

I heard her coming after me.

"Just listen."

She grabbed my shoulder and I spun around, aiming the container of pepper spray right at her eyes. "Dammit, what is your problem?"

I heard her startled intake of breath, saw the shock of betrayal in her eyes. Good. She knew how I felt after she'd worked me over.

DELICIOUSLY DAMAGED

I leaned into her face, my finger on the device. "Stay away from me. I mean it." This time I knew she wouldn't be coming after me.

Lately, leaving Las Vegas sounded better every day.

KB WINTERS

Chapter 14

Savior

"Am I the only one who's on edge when we do these runs?"

That came from the back of the vehicle. Since many of our businesses were cash based, trips to the bank and the credit union were stressful as fuck.

"Hell, no," Cross said from the seat beside me. "If you're not on edge then you've got shit for brains," he said a little louder than necessary to make sure the prospects up front understood. They still had that young man's swagger, thought their shit didn't stink and believed they were immortal. Because they'd made it back from that hell in the desert, they thought they could beat anything. Anyone.

"Don't worry Prez, we're so on edge our assholes are puckering!" Stitch, one of our newest prospects called from behind the wheel.

"Good. Keep 'em puckered. That's how you know you're alive," Cross called out with a gleeful smile. He knew how to fuck with prospects like no one else.

The hummer came to a stop in front of the steps of the credit union and Cross and I jumped out first, carrying the metal boxes of cash straight to the door. Jag was at the doors with Max, holding them open so we wouldn't have to stop. Alonzo, the manager, met us and we went straight back to a secure room.

"Damn that never gets any easier."

"Can I interest you in a coffee while we count, gentlemen?" Alonzo was a well-dressed biracial man with the skinniest fucking moustache I'd ever seen. But he was always polite and professional when we came in, so he was good in my book.

"Coffee sounds good," I told him.

"I'll have tea if you have it," Cross said, shocking the shit out of me.

"Right away," he said, leaving us alone with the cash.

"Tea?"

He shrugged. "I'm trying something new. Gettin' all Zen and shit."

I laughed. "What's her name?"

Cross didn't fuck around like the rest of us, mostly because as Prez, he had the weight of the fucking world on his shoulders. We all helped, but ultimately it was on him to keep us profitable, out of prison and protecting club interests. But still, a man had needs.

"I fucking wish, man. I'm too old to be fucking around with the kind of girls who want to fuck a bad boy. And girls the right age —"

"Don't like to be called girls," I told him with a smirk.

"Smartass. Women the right age don't want to do shit with a biker but fuck him."

"Is it too soon to suggest a Reckless Bitch?"

Cross looked up at me, eyes dark and intense. Then he let out a loud, barking laugh. "You're fucking nuts, Savior."

"Definitely too soon."

Alonzo returned with a coffee and tea, then left with the cash and a promise to return.

"What's going on with you and Mandy?"

"Nothing, so you can save your lecture, all right?"

He raised his hands defensively. "No lecture. I saw you guys at the wedding and you looked cozy. Almost happy."

"Not you, too? A guy spends one weekend with a hot chick and suddenly the whole fucking club thinks I'm about get hitched? What the fuck? Everyone's in love."

"I'd give anything to still be in love, Savior. I wish Lauren was still here, but she's not. She never will be. If you have something, don't piss it away on some macho bullshit."

"Shit, man, I didn't realize." He never talked about his ex. Ever.

"No, it's fine. But watching Max get married after everything he's been through, it has me thinking. Lauren would hate for me to be like this, and fuck man, I'm getting old."

"Hate to break it to you, Prez, but you're already old."

He laughed but his mood was thoughtful. "Don't you ever, I don't know, want. . .*more*?"

"We're all set gentlemen," Alonzo said as he breezed in carrying a few slips of paper. "I have your receipts and your associates have already taken the boxes. Will there be anything else?"

Cross stood and shook the manager's hand. "Nah, we're good. Thank you, Alonzo."

"My pleasure Mr. Cross." The manager held his polite smile, handed Cross the papers and escorted us back to where Jag and Max waited. "Have a good day, gentlemen."

"You too, Alonzo."

Outside the sun hit my skin, warmed it as the anxiety coiled tight in my gut finally started to unwind itself. "Fuck man, I'm too old for this shit."

Cross laughed and fell in step beside me. "If you're too old, what does that make me?"

I glanced at him with a smirk. "In charge."

Max barked out a laugh behind us. "He's got you there, Prez."

Cross looked chagrined, rolling his eyes at us like the little shits we were. "That's right, I am in charge, which means you all need to shut the fuck up."

We all laughed and got back into the hummer. "Where to, Prez?"

"I'm hungry," I told Stitch. "Stop someplace with big burgers, crispy bacon and milkshakes."

"You eat like a ten-year-old," Cross accused.

DELICIOUSLY DAMAGED

I smiled at him. "Cross isn't hungry, Prospect Stitch. Make sure he gets his favorite, the kale and egg salad."

"Asshole," he grunted and I only laughed.

Even though the danger had passed, the tension remained. And I fucking hated tension. "Any word from Gunnar?" I asked, changing the subject.

Gunnar was the Reckless Bastards VP and he'd been MIA for months, checking in sporadically only with Cross.

Cross nodded. "He's just about done settling his mother's estate, but there's some other issues that have cropped up. He should be back in another month or so. I hope."

The stress was probably the reason our Prez was so quiet all the damn time. "Tired of picking up his slack?"

That caught me by surprise. I quickly reassured him, "Fuck no, just curious since you're the only one he calls."

"His head is all fucked up, you know that."

I shook my head. "Our mothers weren't exactly the same, so no, I have no fucking clue."

He leveled me with a look. "Yeah, because little kids who watch their mothers overdose time and time again end up so fucking healthy."

"Never said I was healthy, but thanks for bringing that up, man." My life was no fucking secret but bringing it up like that to prove a fucking point, was a low blow. "Stop the truck," I called out.

"We're not there yet," Stitch shot back.

"I said stop the fucking truck!"

The hummer slowed down and I jumped out.

"Catch you around," I said, slamming the door and walking away. A walk would do me good.

Clear my head, since, according to my own Prez, it was all kinds of fucked up.

***

DELICIOUSLY DAMAGED

"Open up, Mandy!"

Even in my drunken haze, I realized I was loud and obnoxious, and banging on her door like I was an invading army. But like I said, I was drunk with a lot of shit on my mind, including the demons Cross kicked up earlier.

"Mandy!"

The sound of several locks disengaging practically vibrated the door and I stepped back just as Mandy's blonde head appeared between a crack.

"What the hell, Savior?"

She didn't look happy. Yeah, well neither was I. "We need to talk," I yelled into the door.

Her lips were moving but I couldn't hear her words because my gaze was on her swell of cleavage, all creamy and unbound. Tits loose behind the light t-shirt that barely hit mid-thigh.

"It's one in the morning, what could we possibly have to talk about?"

I could tell she wasn't happy to see me. "About why I'm such an asshole," I told her and pushed my way inside. More like stumbling.

"I don't need to know why," she said, but she didn't stop me.

"I owe you that much," I told her because it was true. This wasn't the first time I let Mandy down and my neglect was still impacting her life today, so yeah, I owed her the truth. I just let it rip.

"I have asshole blood in my genes. Dear old dad was long gone before I could even form a memory of his ass, though when Mom got drunk and high, which was all the time, she never passed up an opportunity to tell me just how much I reminded her of him. Then she'd shoot up or snort or smoke a little more until she passed out, sometimes she'd overdose right in front of me."

It was more than sometimes but the truth is that very rarely is the whole truth necessary.

"Holy shit," she sighed, because what else was there to say to something like that? "That's fucked up."

"Yeah, believe me, I know. I barely survived that shit." I let out a long sigh and kicked off my boots, feeling fuzzy and uncomfortable and drunk as fuck. "So now you know. That's my dirty little secret."

I could feel the weight of those green eyes on me and I looked up to see the concern and frustration etched on her face. She shook her head and disappeared into her tiny kitchen, returning with a glass of icy cold water.

"Drink this," she commanded.

After shoving the glass in my hand, she dropped down on the sofa beside me and curled into the other side.

"Thank you for telling me, Savior, but really you don't need to. You don't owe me an explanation and certainly not your whole history."

"I wanted you to know."

"Why?"

That was the fucking question, wasn't it?

Why?

Why did I leave the air-conditioned car with my club brothers, go get drunk at some pub on the main drag and take a cab to Mandy's apartment? No fucking clue.

"Because Cross called me a coward." I told her all about my conversation earlier with the club president. "Why did he have to bring that shit up?" It came out as more of a whine than I wanted it to.

She sat quietly, contemplating her words before she spoke. "Probably to kick your ass into action? Just because your friend Gunnar had a good mother, doesn't make the loss the same. Moms are special, even the shitty moms leave a mark."

"Yours wasn't a shitty mom," I insisted like a pouting child.

"No, not as far as I remember. But she's been gone more of my life than she was around, so I don't have much of an opinion when it comes to the subject."

She didn't sound like it but I didn't want to push. As Cross proved earlier, mothers were a touchy subject. She asked gently, "Why are you all out of sorts over any of this, anyway?"

I shrugged. "Fuck if I know." And that was the kicker. I really had no damn clue what had brought on this bad mood.

She threw her hands up and rolled her eyes. "Well I'm glad I woke up for this. Totally worth the lack of sleep," she grumbled and stood, staring down at me with kind eyes that didn't match the bite in her words.

"Stay here tonight, sleep off the booze. I can take you to your car in the morning but I have to be up and gone early, Savior. Early."

I nodded and stood on shaky legs, bouncing off the walls as I made my way to her bedroom and dropped down onto the bed. "Fuck, I'm hammered."

"Clearly. Delusional, too, if you think you're sleeping in here," she told me as she came inside and climbed on what was obviously her side of the bed based on the rumpled bedding and dented pillow.

"Come on, Pixie. We've already fucked each other inside out and tonight I really am just trying to sleep."

I didn't wait for her to respond. I couldn't. I'd be knocked out in the next few minutes so I stripped down to my underwear and slid beneath the sheets beside her.

"What are you doing?"

"I'm getting comfy," I told her, curling my body around hers so her back was flush with my front. "You're so warm and soft, a sexy little pillow I wish I wasn't too drunk to fuck."

Her husky laugh sounded, vibrating back and forth between our bodies. "Thank God for small favors, then."

"Nothing small about it," I mumbled before burying my face in her neck and drifting off to the best damn sleep of my life.

KB WINTERS

Chapter 15

Mandy

"That feels too good to make you stop, but how can it already be morning?"

Despite the tongue currently painting long strokes around one of my breasts, I felt too tired to be awake and too good to go back to sleep.

"Easy, the sun came up and now its morning," Savior, explained, his blue eyes laughing at me, his tongue tickling over my nipples, one and then the other until I moaned and arched into him. "Besides, I had to wait till morning so I could see how hot you look when I make you feel good."

His words brought a smile to my face. "Then make me feel good, Savior. Really good." The words practically purred out of me when his tongue stroked my body, up and down my midsection, behind my knees and down my belly. Between my thighs.

"Your wish . . ." he said and trailed off as his mouth got down to work on other, more important things. Things like nibbling my inner thigh and swiping his tongue across it to soothe the tingling.

". . . is," he murmured as his thumbs parted my pussy lips and he licked me from my opening to my clit.

". . . my command."

He ravished me, licked at me until I felt like I was climbing the walls, unsure if I wanted him to get closer or pull away.

"So good. Too good," I moaned and sank one hand in his thick brown hair, massaging his scalp while also tugging on his ears. "More."

His laugh sounded through my body, but his tongue moved faster and he added two fingers to the party, gaining intensity and speed until my skin broke out in a sweat. Moans and cries flew from my mouth like a prayer or maybe a song, I didn't know.

All I knew was, nothing in my life had ever felt this damn good.

"You're so close," he growled and stared up at me for a moment, blue eyes intense, mouth slick with my juices. "I can feel those tiny little flutters in your pussy, telling me just how close you are."

He laughed as his thumb circled my clit and I arched into him. "See how much faster you squeeze my fingers when I play with your clit?"

"Yeah, just like that," I panted, unable to look away from the erotic picture he made with that sultry smile. "Oh, shit."

"Yeah, come for me Mandy. You're right there. Just . . . come for me."

And I did. I let the pleasure swamp me, drown me in its weight and depth. My whole body shook as cries vibrated through my body, echoing against the walls. I shook and shook until my body was too spent to do anything other than lie there.

"That was the perfect way to wake me up, Savior," I gasped, "and if you give me a minute, I'll be ready for round two."

His mouth dragged its way up my body, not stopping until he was at my mouth, taking it with as much passion, as much energy as he'd just lavished on my pussy.

"I think you're ready right now," he groaned as he slid between my legs, deep into my body. He was right where he wanted to be, driving deep and hard, going faster and faster as he chased the pleasure that had been building since his tongue began its glorious torture. "So fucking ready," he whispered, and I wasn't sure if he meant me or himself.

It felt good. Better than anything I had ever felt in my whole life. I lost myself in him. I couldn't see or hear or feel anything other than the way he moved inside me with a slow pace that inched my passion up and pushed me closer to orgasm, but not fast enough. "More, please," I pleaded.

Then, my alarm sounded. His deep chuckle sounded in my ear as his tongue swept from my neck up to my ear. "I love to hear you beg."

DELICIOUSLY DAMAGED

"Fuck," I grunted out, frustrated as hell at the impatient buzzing I wanted to ignore, but couldn't. My hand shot out and smacked the alarm.

"Think you can get us there before snooze wears off?"

Savior's grin lit up like a Christmas tree. "Fuck yeah. Challenge accepted."

And he got us there, hard and fast and with a few minutes to spare.

It was the perfect way to start the day. Which meant it only had one place to go.

To shit.

***

Cupcakes. That's what I spent six of my eight-and-a-half-hour shift baking. Fucking cupcakes. Not that I had anything against cupcakes, I didn't. But it was another punishment from Landry, all because I had the audacity to call him on his shitty behavior.

I could have screamed and thrown a tantrum but it wouldn't have done any good. Landry was a complete asshole and would always be one. So I went back to the first day of culinary school and made cupcakes. Butter and chocolate and strawberry. Boring but easy work.

The perfect way to spend the day after the most erotic morning of my life. My body still hummed at the memory of what Savior had done to me. The way his tongue, his fingers and that beautiful, thick cock brought me pleasure was intense. If I had five minutes and some privacy, I could get off just from the memory of his touch.

"Sutton, I need those cupcakes!" His big round body scooted to my work station and grabbed the cupcakes that I had just pulled from the oven.

"About damn time," he grumbled.

"Those are still warm, Chef."

DELICIOUSLY DAMAGED

I knew he heard me because I saw the small hitch in his step but he plowed forward, already preparing the next scathing comment. After cleaning my hands, I leaned against the table and watched as Landry passed several tables filled with already cool cupcakes, perfect to slather on his shitty sugary frosting.

Nevertheless, he took the warm ones straight to his station.

"They don't teach you to let cupcakes cool before frosting them, at fancy New York culinary schools? Perhaps you should have gone to Paris, like I did," he snickered, so fucking proud of his dim wit.

My gaze shot to the clock. Ten minutes left on my shift and then I could say goodbye to this place. For a few hours anyway, though the desire to leave forever grew stronger every shift. Ten minutes without killing my buffoon of a boss and I would make it another day.

"Is your hearing shot, too?" He laughed, looking around and waiting for the others to join in but they didn't. They never did. It always made me laugh.

"Maybe if you weren't so determined to try and humiliate me you wouldn't have wasted a dozen cupcakes fresh from the oven."

It's not like he made the trip all the way over to my station because his fat ass enjoys exercise.

I should have kept my mouth shut but I couldn't help it. I offered, "Or maybe in Paris they don't teach you that cupcakes fresh from the oven shouldn't be frosted right away. Chef."

Two minutes on the clock and I began wiping down my station, ignoring his loud bluster. I was sure I would be without a job soon and I couldn't find it in myself to give a damn. I'd come here to learn from him. Now, it didn't even matter. I knew all I needed to know. He was a mean vile son of a bitch and I didn't need him to advance in my career. Not anymore.

"Where do you think you're going?" he demanded.

I looked up at him, trying to keep attitude out of my glance. "Away from here. My shift is just about over." By the time the stainless steel was clean and dry, it was two minutes past time to go.

"I don't think so. You owe me a dozen cupcakes." Arms crossed, he held an angry scowl as his red face darkened in anger.

I forced a smile to hide my true feelings. "The ones you took were the extra batch. For your mistakes, of course."

There were actually two dozen, but he could figure that out after I was gone.

"Later gators," I called to the rest of the kitchen staff who always seemed amused by my run-ins with Landry.

As soon as the sun hit my face, the tension band holding my shoulders snapped and I could breathe. Finally. As happy as I was to be gone, to be away from Landry so I could press rewind on my morning with Savior, it was just temporary. He hadn't fired me and I hadn't quit, which meant I had to go back tomorrow.

I'd much rather focus on Savior but that wouldn't do me any good. There was nothing to be done about him in the immediate future. Despite what he'd said last night, he'd told me all about his horrible, awful family as a warning. He couldn't or wouldn't give me more, and it didn't matter to him that I hadn't actually *asked* for more. It was a preemptive strike, just in case I got any ideas about him and forever.

As if.

"Mandy, Mandy, Mandy."

Shit. I didn't recognize those voices, which meant they were trouble. The kind of trouble I didn't have the tools or weaponry to deter. My car was still too far away for me to make a run for safety, so I took a few steps forward before turning to face them, my fight or flight senses already kicking in. "Do I know you?" I said to the three assholes with the Roadkill MC patch on their *kuttes.*

"Not yet. Tell us you'll have the money you owe us and you won't have to."

DELICIOUSLY DAMAGED

The blond with the buzz cut acted as spokesperson or maybe it was the jagged scar that ran from the corner of his right eye to his mouth.

"I don't owe you a damn thing, so I guess you got your wires crossed somewhere."

Buzz cut tossed his head back and laughed. "Really? Because Krissy says you're a crack card counter and that's how she's gettin' us what she owes us."

I wasn't a liar but living the way I had as a kid meant I had a damn good poker face. "Well then she told you wrong. I *used* to count cards, about ten years ago. It took a long time to get good at it, more time than you —"

Buzz cut stopped my words with a backhand across my face.

"I didn't ask for your fucking life story, bitch. Tell me you'll have my money."

I shook my head, shaking away the ringing that dulled every sound. "I won't have it. Even if I did play that tournament, I'd never make it past the first round. And that's if they even let me in the casino."

"Shut the fuck up!" His fist came flying again, this time right to my stomach and I doubled over, coughing and struggling to breathe.

"Krissy said you never got caught."

"Well Krissy's a goddamn liar, isn't she?"

I knew he was interested now and I kept talking even as I felt my cheek swelling. "She has no idea why I up and left the city years ago," I told him, thinking as fast as I could before another fist descended.

A snivelly rat with greasy brown hair invaded my space. "She's lying, man. Look at that lying little face." He had a smile like a cartoon villain. "I hate a lying bitch," he crowed and before I could take a step back, he punched me in the face and I hit the ground.

It took a second for my body to realize it had dropped to the hard, hot concrete, but when it did, all I could do was groan in pain. My jaw felt like it was broken in a thousand pieces. My teeth hurt. I wanted to cry and scream and yell. But I wouldn't. Not now. Not ever.

Buzz cut leaned down and hissed like a serpent, "No more fucking excuses, Mandy. Get the fucking money or live with the consequences." He wasn't that close, at least from what I could tell through my non-swollen eye, which happened to be pressed against the ground.

"Or maybe you won't live with them," he added ominously.

I closed my eyes. A few seconds, maybe a few hours passed and then I felt it, a boot in my stomach, on my arm, my back, my face. I curled up into a ball the best I could. Over and over, blow after blow rained down on me until I couldn't move. Could barely see, not that I wanted to open my eyes.

I could only hear the sound of three sets of booted feet stomp away. Buzz cut, Snivelly Rat and some silent asshole, growing farther and farther away as everything around me went black.

***

I don't know how many minutes passed after I lost consciousness. No one had rushed to my aid or even ambled to my aid so when I came to and remembered the attack, I slowly sat up and caught my breath.

Fucking Vegas.

Standing was more of a challenge, and breathing was pure torture. I leaned against the trunk of the nearest car and scanned the parking lot to make sure they were gone. I limped to my car with a swollen eye and an arm I could tell was broken, then managed to slide behind the wheel and get the engine started. My seatbelt wasn't going to happen with this pain. If those dickwads hadn't killed me, I figured my number wasn't up today.

It was the dumbest thing I'd ever done, even dumber than sleeping with Savior and coming back to Vegas all rolled into one, but I drove myself to the hospital. It took longer than it should, given my limited vision and the setting sun, to say nothing of the excruciating pain throbbing throughout my body.

DELICIOUSLY DAMAGED

But I made it.

Mostly.

I left my car parked at an angle in the ambulance bay and staggered inside the hospital before passing out in the arms of a brown-eyed male nurse.

I faded in and out of consciousness but knew it took several people to get me into a room and check me out.

One of them kept asking questions.

"Does she have any I.D.? Anyone we should call?"

The voice belonged to an older woman.

A man answered. *"There are hardly any numbers in her phone. Work. Landlord. Teddy. The rest are just numbers, no names."*

"Just call the one with an actual name," another female voice snapped. Probably the doctor, frustrated as she moved fast, blasting orders, poking my wounds. Annoyed.

Eventually the drugs they gave me kicked in and I couldn't hear them not-so-silently judge me anymore.

Chapter 16

Savior

I felt like a fucking creeper, at worst, a stalker for sitting outside Mandy's place waiting for her to come home. But it was past seven and she worked a long day that started at five in the morning. I wasn't worried and it wasn't like I had the right to call her up and ask here where in the hell she was. So I leaned against my bike in the guest parking spot beside hers and waited.

And waited. When the clock drew closer to eight I began to worry and decided I would swing by *Knead* just to be sure. Before I got settled on my bike, the phone rang.

"Yeah?" I barked, pissed it wasn't Mandy.

"Savior, man, where are you?" Golden Boy's voice sounded weird and instantly I was on edge.

"I'm at Mandy's waiting for her to get home. What's up?"

"Stay where you are. I'm coming to pick you up. Now," he said and ended the call before I could ask any more questions, damn him.

Luckily, I didn't have to wait long before he pulled up in Teddy's Mercedes. When I spotted Teddy in the passenger seat I finally understood what people meant when they said their blood ran cold.

It'd never made much fucking sense before, blood was never cold. It was warm, warmer than you would imagine and when shit got real, it got even hotter. I'd been to war, killed for my government and my club, and never had I been as scared as watching my brother and his pregnant fiancée get out of the car and waddle my way. "What the hell is going on?"

Teddy stepped forward, one hand on my shoulder and the other on her belly. "I just got a call from the hospital. They didn't say much other than Mandy was hurt very badly and mine was the only number in her phone. That's all we know but I thought you'd want to know."

DELICIOUSLY DAMAGED

I nodded but my mind was blank and racing too fast to do anything else but bark, "Let's go!"

I grabbed Teddy's arm and helped her back into the car before jumping in the backseat while I thought of what "hurt very badly" meant with the shit going on with her friend and those fuckers from the parking lot.

I was ready to kill the motherfuckers.

At the hospital, there was more fucking waiting and no answers. It was nearly ten by the time someone with a stethoscope around his neck came out to update us on Mandy's condition. His gaze focused on Teddy, who'd been vocal in wanting, no *demanding* progress.

"Ms. Sutton has a fractured ulna and radius, bruised ribs along with a nasty black eye. Those are the big injuries, but she has quite a few scrapes and bruises all over. The good news is that she'll recover."

"And the bad news?" Teddy took a step closer, her gaze focused and intense.

"We don't know what happened to her," the doctor said. "She drove herself in that condition, leaving her car in the ambulance area. The nurse has her keys," he told them and Golden Boy left to move it.

"Can we see her, doctor?" Teddy looked so damn worried I thought she might end up going into labor early.

"I'm sorry miss but she is heavily sedated and probably won't be awake for hours. We're going to keep her for at least one night to monitor for concussion. We think she lost consciousness when she sustained her injuries but we're not sure. That could mean head trauma. If she was knocked out, she doesn't know for how long and we haven't been able to keep her awake long enough to get any more details."

With a polite smile, the doctor walked away.

I couldn't let that ride, though. I needed more. Not only was I worried as shit but would Ammo kick my ass from here to hell for leaving her without making sure she was okay.

"Hey, Doc!" I caught up with him in the hall and he flashed a worried grin.

DELICIOUSLY DAMAGED

"How can I help you, Mister . . .?"

"Call me Vick, please." Sometimes I forgot how we looked to normal people. "Doc, I'm a family friend of Mandy's but the problem is she's lost all her family. I served with her brother and he didn't make it back after his last tour."

I ran completely out of steam and my shoulders fell, thinking about how I'd let Ammo down. Let Mandy down.

"Say no more, Vick. I was a combat medic and I get it. Follow me."

With a grateful smile, I followed him down a long corridor to a small, antiseptic room with too many machines for Mandy's little body. I ached for her and the pain she must be feeling based on the strain on her face. "Thanks, Doc. I promise to stay out of the way, I just want to be here when she wakes up."

When the doctor left, I texted Teddy and Golden Boy to let them know I was with Mandy, got settled in a damned uncomfortable hard plastic chair. And waited.

And waited.

And fucking waited.

Finally, around two in the morning those pretty green eyes popped open and I could breathe again.

Chapter 17

Mandy

"Do you really have to do this now? She's been awake for five fucking minutes!" I could hear Savior's angry voice and I doubted he was talking to the doctors or nurses like that.

"Sir, your girlfriend was the victim of a crime, don't you want us to find the perpetrators. If there are even perpetrators," a taunting voice said that I assumed belonged to one of Vegas' finest.

Insert eye roll if you want.

I appreciated Savior fighting for me, but it was unnecessary. I woke up some time in the middle of the night, not that the rest was all that peaceful with the nurses waking me up every hour to ask me ridiculous questions: What day is it? Who's the president? Two questions guaranteed to piss me off. Somehow I came out of that fracas with no brain damage, just a few bruises, cuts and fractures that would keep me out of work for who knew how long. Maybe I'd find out if the doctor ever made his way to this side of the hospital.

"I'm awake," I called out to stop the damn pissing contest outside my door.

The door opened and Savior popped his head in, blue eyes looking stark against his pale skin and dark hair. "How are you feeling?"

"Not as good as I would be if two gorillas weren't yelling outside my door." And if I hadn't gotten my ass stomped by a bunch of pissed off bikers. "Come on in and bring your friend."

His lips twitched but Savior refused the smile and stepped inside, not bothering to hold the door for the two men I pegged as detectives based on their suits. One wore an ill-fitting brown suit like a cop from the seventies and the other, well he looked like a mob lawyer.

"They want to ask you some questions," he said reluctantly and sat in the chair where I found him when I woke up.

"Alone," mob lawyer said with a frown.

"He wasn't involved so I'd rather he stay." I didn't like cops and I didn't trust them, but I knew they were only doing their jobs right now. Still, I needed backup and Savior was it. He grabbed my hand and gave it a squeeze to let me know he was there.

The detectives stood at the foot of the bed wearing twin scowls meant to intimidate. "Can you tell us what happened, Ms. Sutton?"

I nodded and let out a sigh, wincing as the pain lit up my ribcage.

"Shit that hurts!" I yelled without thinking. I guessed my ribs didn't get the memo that they weren't broken because those fuckers *hurt*. "I was leaving work when three guys approached me in the parking lot of *Knead*, it's the restaurant where I work. They had on jackets that said Roadkill MC, if that helps." I paused because talking and breathing? Not so easy to do with bruised ribs, it turned out.

Seventies detective looked at me with a look of disbelief. "What business do you have with them?"

I barked out a laugh that was worth the fucking pain. "I have no business with them, but someone I knew when I lived here as a kid promised them I would do something I don't do anymore." I flashed a look at the detectives and then at Savior. There was no point trying to hide it anymore. It would come out anyway. "A woman I knew back when I was a kid, she helped me get a fake ID when my brother's tour in Afghanistan was extended. I needed to pay bills, get food and stuff."

"Where were your parents," mob lawyer asked.

"Dead, for years at this point. Anyway, I saw this video online about counting cards and it seemed easy enough. I trained myself to do it and I only took enough to pay the bills and have some cushion, but Krissy wanted more."

Mob lawyer interrupted me, giving me a chance to slow down and ease the pain. "Who's Krissy?"

I hadn't made it clear? "The so-called friend who got me the ID. She wanted a cut in exchange for the favor."

His eyebrows rose in understanding as if I'd finally explained nuclear fission to him. So I continued.

"After a while it became too much, too risky. I got my acceptance letter for culinary school, hopped on a bus and never looked back." I sighed deeply a few times, to breathe through the pain. "Until I returned six months ago to bury my brother and then three months later when I took the job at *Knead*."

Both of them nodded as they jotted down notes. "And the beat down?"

"Encouragement to sign up for the blackjack tournament at the Wynn." My head dropped back on the pillow and I focused on keeping my breathing even for a few long moments. That shit hurt and bad, but if

I answered their questions now, I wouldn't have to see them again.

"They just came up to you one day and asked you to count cards for them and then showed up a few weeks later to do this to you?" Mob lawyer pointed at me, or specifically, my injuries, suspicion lacing his words.

"No, they came by a few times to convince or intimidate me, whatever you want to call it."

"And you didn't think to call the police?"

"For what? So you can accuse me of some shit I had no part in? Right."

"Except you did," he countered.

"As a minor and you can't prove it. But if you want to try, go ahead. Just don't contact me, contact my lawyer."

Seventies Detective cleared his throat and glared at the younger man. "That's not necessary, Ms. Sutton. You're the victim."

"Really? Because I think someone failed to tell your partner." I turned my head away. "I don't know the guys' names. What I know is that Krissy owes them money, a few hundred grand. Now I'm done talking."

"We have more questions."

I stared at Mob Lawyer until he shrugged, gave up and walked away.

"Most victims want our help, Ms. Sutton."

I rolled my eyes at the line cops always dragged out when they wanted more information than they had. "Intimidating victims isn't the best way to get us to open up, and somehow I knew that counting cards at sixteen would be all you heard."

He seemed sympathetic, but I was pretty sure they taught that look at the police academy. "Are we planning to handle this ourselves," he asked, brown eyes directed squarely at Savior, who'd been surprisingly quiet, if tense as hell beside me.

"Not if we don't have to." They stared at each other, some kind of macho mental pissing contest before Seventies Detective walked away.

This was my life now. Two men standing on either side of me, talking about me like I wasn't there. Wounded in a hospital bed because of some chick I used to know and this was the perfect excuse for Landry to fire me.

Facing charges for the old card counting schemes didn't worry me. I didn't need a get-out-of-jail card—I needed a get-out-of-town card.

Chapter 18

Savior

"Shit Mandy, I'm sorry."

What else could I say after hearing everything, all laid out like a hand of cards for the cops? If I had a heart, it would've broken for her. For the shit she'd gone through when I promised to look out for her, for all the losses she suffered and for the pain written all over her face. She was stronger than even she knew, protecting herself the best she knew how even when it got her hurt.

"Not your fault," she said, trying for flippant, but it came out tired. Frustrated.

"Maybe, maybe not." I couldn't have her let me off that easy. "But it is in a way because I should have been there for you when you were a kid. If I had been, you wouldn't have needed to do what you did to survive."

She rolled her eyes, ready to make light of the situation. "It was counting fucking cards, dude, not selling my ass."

I huffed out a laugh. "Things might have been easier if you had. You think the casino owners would've cared that you were a teenager?" They wouldn't have and thinking about what they would have done to her if she'd been caught, made me want to fucking puke. "I really am sorry."

"For fuck's sake Savior, I was never your responsibility. Whatever promise you made to Ammo, forget it. He's not here to kick your ass or haunt you, or whatever has you so worried."

"According to you, but I made a promise to your brother and I fucked that up."

She shot me a grin, full of sarcasm. "As long as it's all about you."

"Of course." I spread my arms wide with a confident grin, inviting her to look me over until she did. Thoroughly and with heat in her eyes. "Watch it, Pixie. You're too hurt to be looking at me like that."

"Never too hurt to look, babe." She grinned and her gaze slid up and down my body one final time. "Look, Savior, I know you feel guilty about whatever you feel guilty about but you don't need to stick around here. I'm fine but they're worried about a concussion, so I'll probably be here another night or two."

"You're kicking me out?" I spent the past twelve hours sleeping in a hard ass chair at her side and she didn't even want me here.

"No." She tried to readjust her position and let loose a string of swear words that would make a Ranger blush. "I'm saying that if you're here out of obligation or guilt, I'm not interested."

"I'm here because hearing you'd been hurt took about a decade off my life. I thought for sure I was about to hear that . . ."

I couldn't even finish the thought, it was too hard. To fucking hard to think about.

"I'm fine, Savior. Just a few scrapes and bruises."

"And a fractured ulna and radius. Sorry to tell you, Pixie, but you don't look fine."

She fluffed her tangled short hair with her good hand and stuck out her lips in that way chicks loved to do when they took selfies. "You mean I'm not giving Teddy a run for her money?"

"You know you're beautiful, Mandy. But you've got one eye almost swollen shut and the best part of you is covered in a cast and bandages. Kind of dims the beauty." She was stunning and had no damn idea. It was a shame she didn't have people in her life constantly telling her how amazing she was.

"Yeah well, you try taking who knows how many boot kicks to the body and let's see how pretty you look."

"Shit, Mandy. I'm going to kill those fuckers."

"Get in line. I get the first hit, maybe the first ten." Her expression sobered. "What can I do?"

I stood and dropped a kiss to her hair. "Get some rest. I'm going to let the guys know what's going on and see what else we can find out."

She nodded but she had already checked out, her gaze focused on a fixed point on the wall, glazed over.

"Mandy?"

She blinked and looked up at me. "Yeah?"

"It's not obligation or responsibility or even guilt. Ammo will always be one of us, which means so will you."

I found Teddy and Jana in the waiting room with three large bags filled with crap. "Hey ladies, she's awake, grouchy and in need of female company."

"Perfect." Jana tried to stand and I went to help her. "Thanks, this baby is screwing up my center of gravity."

"Should either of you be here with all these germs?"

Teddy scowled at me and poked me in the center of the chest. "We'll be fine, Savior. You go do whatever you need to get those dark shadows out of your eyes. Mandy might not know it yet, but she needs you."

I nodded and walked them to the elevator, Teddy's words ringing in my head on a loop. Despite what she'd said, I had a feeling I needed Mandy even more.

***

"It was Roadkill MC. Mandy saw the fucking patches before they stomped on her." Now that I was free of the hospital and watchful eyes, my rage was on full fucking display. What they did to her wasn't right. That's not how you treat women, especially innocent women. "Some bitch she used to hang with back in the day owes them a lot of money."

DELICIOUSLY DAMAGED

Cross sat in his spot at the head of the table, arms crossed and a scowl on his face. "You're sure Mandy doesn't owe this money to them for something?"

His implication was clear and the only reason I didn't leap over the table and wrap my hands around his fucking neck was because he was my brother. My Prez.

"I'm damn sure." I sighed, trying to figure out how much to tell without breaking Mandy's confidence. "She knew this woman as a kid, when Ammo was re-upped before he even got stateside. She had no money and no way to get any." I didn't want to tell them, but I needed my club right now. Mandy was . . . fuck if I knew, but she was *something* to me and I needed everybody's help to keep her safe. So I told them about the card counting and about that bitch Krissy. All of it.

"Card counting? That little bitty thing with the short blond hair?" Lasso's wide smile was filled with disbelief. "As a kid?"

"A teenager, fifteen to seventeen I think, before she left for school." Cross still stared at me and I stared back. "We should have been looking out for her back then. If we'd done what the fuck we were supposed to, she wouldn't be in this shit today."

He knew I was right even if he didn't like being called out like that.

"You're right," he finally admitted, looking as deflated as the rest of us old timers who knew Ammo and his loss and the little girl in his care. It was why he'd joined the military and the Reckless Bastards. All for her. "What do you want to do, Savior?"

I smiled. "What I'd like to do is kill those motherfuckers who did this to her, but I'd settle for a beat down."

"Or we could give those assholes something else to worry about." Jag's bright white smile shone like the goddamn sun when he was being devious. "Nothing illegal, just some shit guaranteed to fuck up their week. Make them focus on something other than our Mandy."

DELICIOUSLY DAMAGED

I gave Jag a short nod. He was one of a fucking kind, embracing Mandy like she was already part of the Reckless Bastards, because she was.

"Thanks, man. We need to hit them hard and let them know why without starting a goddamn war."

Then Stitch butted in. "I heard they got a new shipment of girls and stashed them all at a house in the 'burbs." Stitch, always a good time guy, didn't have his usual smile and I knew he was as pissed as the rest of us even if he didn't know Ammo.

I leaned forward, eager for more information. "Where'd you hear that?"

He grinned. "One of the blue hairs who comes into the dispensary told me her neighbors just brought a bunch of scrawny girls who all looked Russian to the old Victorian on her block." He pulled his phone from his pocket and slid it to me. "She gave me the address of the house and the cross street. Said if something was done about it, she'd bake us some of her snickerdoodles with pot in 'em." Stitch leaned back and sneered with that grin of his. "Sounded like a good idea, but your thing is more urgent."

We brainstormed ideas for more than an hour before Cross ended the meeting. "I need to think about this for a minute. Church tomorrow at noon. Be there," he said and we all dispersed.

I had one more thing I needed to do before I went back to the hospital, back to Mandy. Despite what she'd said, I would be there by her side until she could stand on her own again. Maybe longer if she stopped being so damn stubborn.

Max rested a hand on my shoulder and fell in step beside me. "Hey man, you okay?"

"Fucking peachy, man."

"Don't do something stupid right now."

I glared but he only glared back, stoic bastard that he was.

"Believe me," he said in that soft and easy voice you use when you're worried about a friend. "I'd be right beside you, busting up flesh if I thought it was the right move. But right now Mandy is defenseless and she knows you better than any of us. She needs you."

I brushed off his concern with a quick, "The last thing she needs is me, trust me on that." For some reason his advice got under my skin and didn't do anything to ease the guilt eating away my gut. Maybe logically he was right but it didn't work for me right now. What I needed to do was focus on getting those Roadkill assholes for what they did.

"You sound like a dumbass," Max said with all the affection of a grumpy older brother. "You are exactly what she needs. Are you really so blind you can't see it?"

"See what?" I snapped. "That if I'd kept my promise to Ammo all those fucking years ago, she wouldn't be in this fucked up mess right now? I see that loud and clear. Trust me on that one."

"I do trust you, Savior. With my life, but you need to trust *me* on this. I nearly lost Jana because my head was so far up my ass."

"That was PTSD," I huffed out angrily. "Not exactly the same thing."

We'd reached the parking lot. Max laughed and hopped on his bike, parked beside mine. "Wrong, it's exactly the same fucking thing, man. You think your life, your childhood and your time in the military didn't leave its mark? If so, you're dumber than you look."

"Fuck you, I look good as shit."

"Whatever you need to tell yourself, Savior." He started his bike and adjusted his helmet. I didn't even bother watching him ride off. There was one more brother I had to see.

The winding road curved left and right between big, lush trees that somehow managed to remain a vibrant green in the desert. I parked my bike and found the spot I was looking for. It looked different than I thought it would, but I don't know what I was expecting since visiting cemeteries wasn't how I spent my free time. But Ammo had been here for too damn long and my visit was long overdue.

DELICIOUSLY DAMAGED

I squatted down in front of his shiny black headstone. "Hey man. Sorry I haven't been back since your funeral but life, ya know?" I felt like a jackass talking to him like this, but I needed to do it. "I'm sorry, man. So fucking sorry that I didn't look out for Mandy the way I should have. I could make excuses, blame it on being young and dumb, but it would be nothing but a fucking excuse."

I knew by then I had a lot more to say to him, a lot more to think about. I slid down onto my ass and got more comfortable, like I was just talking to an old friend. I let him down and by extension, Mandy. And to make me an even bigger asshole, I slept with her. More than once. I wasn't sure how I could explain all that, but I had to try.

"She's been through some shit man, a lot of shit. More than someone her age should, but she turned out amazing. Tough and beautiful, strong and brave, and she doesn't even know how damn special she is. It's a nice change from your gigantic fucking ego." I laughed.

Actually laughed in a cemetery. Where my best friend would rest forever.

I didn't know how long I sat there in the grass, my arms resting on my knees, talking to Ammo. Laughing with him and catching up on the Reckless Bastards. "Golden Boy is finally out of prison, scot free and engaged to a model if you can believe it. Max had a beach wedding in San Diego, and it was nicer than it sounds."

I told him about Gunnar's mom dying, Cross drinking tea, Golden Boy's tattoo parlor and even the shit going down with those Roadkill fuckers. "I'm doing my best, man. I won't let her or you down again."

I sat in the cemetery just watching all the different flowers as they blew in the wind, all of them left lovingly by friends and family of the dead. I didn't even know if my mom was alive or dead, hell my deadbeat dad either. They could both be still roaming this earth or rotting inside it and I wouldn't know either way because they didn't matter to me. They weren't my family. Ammo was my family and I'd treated him no better than my own mother, putting my needs first, consequences be damned.

I stood and swiped away grass and dirt I didn't see but felt the need to clean off anyway. My mind was full, wondering how Mandy was doing. If she was feeling frustrated or suffocated by all the love coming from Jana and Teddy. Wondering if she was really doing okay or if she was putting up a front, something I now knew she could do so well.

It was a damn shame that I had to give her up because she needed someone better than me in her life. She deserved someone better than I could ever hope to be and I knew that. I wasn't cut out to be an old man to a hot chick. My mind was too fucked up. I could fuck her, and I could protect her. But true love and frou-frou relationships were out of my league.

And the moment that thought went through my mind, I realized exactly how much I wanted her.

KB WINTERS

Chapter 19

Mandy

"We got you tons of stuff to keep you occupied until they spring you."

Teddy beamed a smile as she and Jana unpacked the bags they set on the edge of my hospital bed.

I smiled as I watched them work in tandem, pulling out a stack of magazines, leave-in conditioner and a brush, moisturizer and a tablet.

"Wow," was all I could say at their generosity, and even that hurt my ribs.

"The tablet is mine," Jana said sheepishly, "but I know how hard it can be cooped up in here without anything to entertain you." Her hand instinctively went to the scar along one side of her face. It wasn't really noticeable until she drew attention to it, but we all had our quirks, so who was I to judge?

They were so cheerful, so upbeat that it made me suspicious. "What's going on? Do you know something I don't, like I'm dying or there's a contract on my life?"

Teddy and Jana stared at each other with twin serious expressions and then promptly burst out laughing. "Sorry to break it to you Mandy but you're going to live. This is called friendship. You need us, so we're here. To help you forget just how much life sucks right now."

That pulled a laugh from me.

"Understatement of the . . . well, fucking ever," I managed to say before I had to count to ten to absorb the pain.

I shouldn't be surprised about the shit show my life was now; it wasn't like there had ever been a break when things were perfect. Hell, not even perfect. I'd have settled for uneventful. Boring, even. But that wasn't the life lined up for me. "It does suck and I appreciate you bringing these things to me but I'm sure you both have better things to do than hang out here for the second day in a row."

DELICIOUSLY DAMAGED

I had no clue when they would let me out and I hadn't made a big deal about it yet because it didn't matter to me where I was at the moment.

"See that's where you're wrong," Teddy said with a sassy point of her finger. "We're pregnant and hungry, and if one of these babies decided to come early, we're right where we need to be." She flashed that tough girl grin that was so far from the high fashion model she'd been that she was like a whole new person.

I appreciated her attempt to keep things light. "And I thought you were here just for me. I'm just a convenience," I told her with a fake sniffle. "Thanks, seriously."

"Don't!" Jana held her hands up in my direction. "We're here for you. You're our friend and we want to be yours but if you keep that up you'll have two pregnant women blubbering like babies in here."

"Thanks for the heads up," I told her, wincing as I tried to sit up.

"How are you feeling, really?" Teddy tilted her head to the side in that classic sign of pity that people thought was sympathy.

"Never better," I told her flippantly. "Doesn't matter, it'll heal. Eventually."

"I'm glad to hear that. Savior looked like he wanted to rip someone's head off when we picked him up," Teddy said. "He's got it bad."

I shook my head, refusing to listen. Maybe that's how women talked when they were together but I didn't want to hear it. "He's got a bad case of guilt and obligation. That's all it is."

They both laughed like it was the funniest damn joke in the world. Teddy blurted out, "Oh Jana, she actually believes that."

I glared at Teddy but it had no effect on the girl.

"It's true, Teddy. He feels bad he didn't look after me like he promised my brother. Thinks all of this is his fault."

DELICIOUSLY DAMAGED

If there was one thing I hated, it was pity. And obligation. I was used to both and neither had ever done a damn thing to make me or my life any better.

"Don't worry," I told them as sleep slowly pulled me under. "I'm fine on my own."

***

When I woke up some time later, the doctor was staring at me with a creepy but professional smile. "Good news Mandy. We're letting you out today."

"Great." I could go home to my tiny apartment and do absolutely nothing with a broken arm and sore ribs.

Then came more good news. "Unfortunately, you will be in that cast for at least six to ten weeks. No work at all during that time, and we'll discuss it more when you're well enough to start therapy." More good news as he spoke. No work. No cooking. No laughing or fucking. No living.

Nothing.

"Super." I murmured.

He gave me a sympathetic smile that made me want to scream. "You're young, Mandy. There's no reason you won't heal completely if you commit to it. I'll get that paperwork started if you want to call someone to pick you up."

"Do you have my phone?" I hadn't thought about it before now because I didn't need it, then the nurse who was checking my vitals pulled a large plastic bag from the closet.

"Here you go dear. If you need anything else, buzz me."

"Thank you." My voice was soft, broken in gratitude as I watched them both leave. Despite my complaining, they'd done so much for me. Yet, I was alone again and though it was the way I'd spent most of my life, it now felt stifling and uncomfortable. So loud and in my face about how alone I was.

But there was nothing to be done about it because despite what Jana and Teddy thought, Savior's absence told me everything.

DELICIOUSLY DAMAGED

I picked up my phone, grateful to whoever had powered it off, and placed a reservation for a cab ride in two hours. It was how I'd always gotten around until I'd bought a car when I moved back to Vegas. I was used to it. Completely self-sufficient.

Because, well, I had to be.

And the more I thought about it, the more leaving Las Vegas sounded just about perfect. Relying on people, making connections was great, for other people. But I was worried that relying on people might make me forget who I was.

Strong.

Capable.

Alone.

***

"I know you're in there, Pixie. Open up!" Savior's voice came out loud enough to drown out the comedy special playing on TV but the pounding on the door shook the walls. "I've got all day."

I let out a long sigh at the thought of getting up. The pain pills worked but not enough. I'd spent the past two days only moving when absolutely necessary. I'd put off going to the bathroom or the kitchen until I couldn't stand it any longer, and I slept in the same spot I was now sitting in on my sofa. "Go away, Savior."

"No. Don't make me break this door down."

That's just what I needed, to get kicked out before I planned to move out anyway. I'd already given my landlord my thirty-day notice but I knew I'd need every one of those days to stay put with my injuries.

I sucked in a long, deep breath and let it out slowly as I stood and made my way to the door. I flipped the lock and twisted the knob before turning back to the sofa. My skin was already damp from the effort it took to breathe deeply and stand. Though my eye was no longer swollen shut, a good thing, the huge, ugly green and yellow bruise didn't do me any favors.

DELICIOUSLY DAMAGED

"What do you want?" I called to him as I made my way back to my cocoon.

"I brought you a few things."

I was busy getting myself settled on the couch again and didn't look at him, at the smile I heard in his voice. I hadn't seen him in a few days and hadn't planned on seeing him again. "I have everything I need but thank you."

When I finally looked up he froze and stared at me with a confused and hurt look on his face. "I'm sorry I haven't been around lately."

I eased back into the couch, waiting for the pain to settle after all that movement. "Don't be. I told you before, not your responsibility." I didn't want to be anyone's responsibility or another item on their list of things they had to do. By now, I knew that's how he would always see me.

"It's not that, I —"

I cut him off. "It's fine, Savior. You have a life and I don't need an explanation, but I do appreciate the thought."

"Goddamn, you are one frustrating woman," he groaned and dropped the bags on the tiny two-legged table that passed off as a dining table. "I went to see Ammo."

Of course he did, because his guilt had probably overwhelmed him and now he was determined to double down on the overprotective thing. "Good for you."

"Did I do something to piss you off, Pixie?"

"Nope. I'm not pissed off. I'm in pain, Savior."

"Do you need pills or water or something?"

I glanced at the case of bottled water under the coffee table and the pills on top of it, then back at him. "I'm good, thanks. Look, Savior, I don't need a babysitter."

"Good, because I'm no one's babysitter. Can't I just do something nice because I want to?"

DELICIOUSLY DAMAGED

"Sure," I told him but I didn't believe him at all.

He was determined to prove me wrong by unpacking the bags and bringing me a plate piled with fried chicken, spaghetti and salad. Before I could complain about how I was going to eat and hold my plate with only one good arm, he raced into my kitchen and returned with my tray table. "See? It's not so bad having me around."

"I never said it was."

"But you implied it." He stared at me again, waiting for a reaction but I had no reaction to give. The pain was so unbearable that I pushed down everything else, all of my thoughts and emotions that had nothing to do with my immediate plans. I couldn't handle anything else.

Not even Savior.

"I'm not going to argue with you," I said and picked up the plastic fork he'd provided.

"No? Then what are you going to do about your friend and Roadkill MC?"

I shrugged. "Nothing."

"That's not going to work, Pixie." His gaze was hard and cold, deadly serious as he sat beside me with his own plate in his hands.

"Well it's the best I can do, so you need to deal with it." I dropped my fork on the plate in frustration. Eating left handed was difficult and leaning forward to do so only made the pain in my ribs worse. Fucking bikers.

"What about your job?"

I laughed bitterly. "What job?"

Landry had been only too happy to learn I wouldn't be back but he wasn't all laughs when he learned I'd been attacked in his parking lot. I could have told him I'd be long gone before I had a chance to sue but he didn't deserve it. Let the fucker stew on it for a while.

"Shit, Mandy. I'm sorry to hear that."

"Don't be. I'm fine with it."

DELICIOUSLY DAMAGED

"What will you do for work?"

I shrugged, for some reason I couldn't tell him the truth, that I would leave and find a job and a home in another city. I couldn't tell him that I was starting over somewhere else and I didn't know why. "Figure it out. It's what I do."

"And Roadkill? You can't really think they'll just let this go, even if you did something crazy like leave town they'd come and find you."

I didn't think that, but I couldn't worry about it. "All they can do is kill me, Savior."

"Don't fucking say that!" He threw his half empty plate on the coffee table with a clatter as his voice echoed in the small room. "That's not funny, Mandy. There's no coming back from that."

"Believe me, I know."

"So this is what, some suicide mission?" He was angry and worried, but I didn't need that from him. Not now.

"No, Savior. I have no desire to die but I can't live my life worrying about them. I can't control what they do, only what I do."

"And what do you plan to do, Mandy?"

"Figure it out. I've got time."

Twenty-eight days to be exact, but that was no one's business but my own.

Chapter 20

Savior

I headed back to the clubhouse to find a quiet corner to get my head straight. Mandy was hiding something from me, but I didn't know what. Not yet, anyway. But I'd figure it out. It was normal for her to feel scared and paranoid after what had happened to her but this was more than that. She didn't want to see me, but not in an angry vengeful way. It was more that she was pulling away from me, withdrawing.

"Earth to Savior. What's going on with you, man?"

I looked up at Cross who wore a worried look that pissed me off. I wasn't some head case he needed to be concerned about. "Shit's going on with me but maybe if you braid my hair and ask again, I'll tell you."

"Asshole. I know this is about what happened to Mandy and I hope you're not planning to do anything stupid."

Even if I wanted to, it would be pointless. She wouldn't listen to me anyway. "I'm not fuckin' planning anything."

He stared at me, waiting for me to crack. But he'd have to wait a long fucking time. "You don't want to talk? Fine. Just listen. Something is clearly going on with you two but you're here at the clubhouse drinking in the middle of the goddamn day instead of being over there with her. She's fucked up man, broken, bruised and battered. And alone. Again."

"Yeah well, she doesn't want me or my help. Thinks I'm her babysitter."

"Have you told her any different?"

"Nah, it's better this way anyway."

"Holy shit. Holy fucking shit." Cross began to laugh and then he laughed harder, clapping me on the back as tears damn near streamed down his face. "How fucking stupid are you, man? You like her."

I shook my head and reached for the bottle, pouring another shot.

DELICIOUSLY DAMAGED

"No, you're right. You don't like her, you *love* her."

I barked out a laugh. "I'm not capable of that particular emotion, brother."

"Tell that shit to someone who doesn't know you. You might be hard as hell on the outside but you know how to love and you love hard. Guys like us, that's how we do it. That's how we can take up arms and fight for this country, fight for the Reckless Bastards. Our love runs deep."

I took another sip of my drink, savoring the amber liquid as I tried to shake off his assessment of me. Not buying it. "Then maybe you ought to get out there and get some of that deep love so you stop trying to play the fucking matchmaker."

He snorted, "If it was that fucking easy, I would. But what you want is right in front of you. If you stop being such a pussy and go after it."

"Yeah, thanks Prez. Always a pleasure talkin' to you."

He laughed. "Asshole."

"That's what they call me."

His bootsteps clattered loud on the hard floor as he walked away, probably back to his office where he spent all of his time. Hiding from life. Avoiding everything to do with living but the club.

But he was right about one thing, Mandy was injured and alone. No matter how much she didn't want me around, she needed me. And I needed to be there for her.

No, I wanted to.

When I pulled into Mandy's parking lot there was one of those big ass yellow charity trucks parked in my spot. Well, in her visitor's spot, but I was so used to parking there it felt like mine. I parked in Mandy's spot and went in search of the guys in blue coveralls, shocked to find them inside Mandy's apartment. "What the hell is going on in here?" A prickle of unease slid down my back, making my skin pucker in awareness. I should have realized something was up when I took her parking space. She had no job and she was still injured, where in the hell was she?

DELICIOUSLY DAMAGED

A guy with curly blond hair who couldn't have been more than twenty-one looked at me with a frown. "We got a call from the tenant and instructions to clear out some stuff. Is anything in here yours?"

I shook my head but still took the clipboard just to make sure this was Mandy's doing and not someone else's. It was her block writing, straight and efficient, with curt instructions.

"Nah, nothing here is mine. This was my friend's place, you know?"

He flashed an understanding smile. "No worries, man. She left as soon as we got here."

And it didn't take a genius to figure out that she'd made good on her threat to leave Las Vegas. I'd thought it was an idle threat, something she blurted out when she was frustrated with her job, her life. Why didn't she tell me she was serious? She left behind everything that was too big to carry, including her television, sofa and bed. She was traveling light, probably to put as much distance between her and Vegas and the Roadkill MC as possible.

The question was, where the hell would she go? Mandy could be any fucking where, headed anywhere and I had no clue where to start looking. "How long ago did she leave?"

The blond looked at his watch and frowned. "About thirty, maybe forty minutes ago. She left instructions and booked it out of here. Only let me carry her bag because I insisted."

"And called her ma'am," one of the other movers, a chubby guy with a red buzz cut said with a wide grin.

"Yeah, she didn't appreciate it," he confirmed with a sheepish grin that told me she'd probably used a few colorful words to express her displeasure.

"Thanks guys." My boots pounded loudly on the concrete steps and I had my phone out, dialing the one person who might have an idea of where she might go, or even better, where she was headed. "Teddy, do you have any idea where Mandy would go if she was leaving town?"

"What?" Her voice screeched so loud I had to pull the damn phone back.

"Teddy, focus. I'm at her place now and the Salvation Army people are here taking all the shit she left behind. Do you know where she went?"

"Shit, I didn't think she was serious. I haven't talked to her in a few days. She hasn't been answering my texts." She went silent as if coming her memory. "You know, last time we did talk, she said maybe it was time she left Vegas. I thought it was the painkillers. She never said she was leaving though." Teddy sounded just as frantic as I felt and that wasn't helping. At all, dammit.

"And you didn't tell me? What the fuck is going on?"

Teddy sighed and I could practically see her rolling her eyes even through the phone. "I don't know, Savior. Maybe she wants to get away from, well, everything."

Ouch. "Yeah, well that's just too damn bad." She would get my help and my protection, along with the rest of the Reckless Bastards. "If you think of anywhere she might go, let me know," I told her and ended the call before she said another word. I hopped on my bike and headed to the clubhouse.

Right now, the only thing I needed was a drink and my brothers.

Chapter 21

Mandy

Why I decided that leaving the city while I still had broken and bruised bones was a good idea, I'd never know. More importantly, I had to question my own smarts when I chose to hop on the I-15 south to Los Angeles. It was a little over a four-hour drive and a few freeways and driving with one hand wasn't the smartest plan I'd ever come up with, but at least I was still breathing.

LA was so damn expensive, plus, traffic was atrocious. On the other hand, it was a great place to get lost for a while. With millions of people in the city and more flooding the limits every day hoping to become the next big thing, I would be just another anonymous face in the crowd. That meant I could heal properly and figure out what came next.

If I ever made it. God, I was stupid to think I could. Not that making the best decisions was my forte or anything.

Pain seared through my midsection and shot up my arm all the way to my skull. After about a half hour of driving, it was so bad I pulled over and closed my eyes. Deep breathing wasn't helping me right now. I contemplated taking a painkiller but I knew if I did I'd be zoned out in the scorching desert heat for hours. Chances were my little piece of shit car would overheat and I'd never get the hell out of here.

It took almost an hour of praying to whoever was up there and long deep breaths before the pain dropped from a nine to a six and I figured that was probably as good as it was going to get. If only I could get my body to listen, to sit up so I could strap the damn seatbelt back on and get back on the road. To yet another temporary stop on my way to my real life.

Whatever the hell that meant.

"Holy shit!" The tap on my window was loud and scared the hell out of me. I looked up and found

Detective Haynes' green eyes peering down at me through the window. When my heart finally decided to stop trying to kill me, I let the window down. "What can I do for you, detective?"

"Going somewhere?"

I huffed out a laugh. "Yeah, trying to escape the biker gang that beat me to a pulp. It may be hard for you to remember since you guys don't give a shit." He flashed that annoyed cop look that did nothing to stop my frustration.

"We need to talk to you, Ms. Sutton." His voice might have scared me if cops didn't always use that tone to get their way. So I said nothing.

"Preferably at the station."

I nodded and tried to get out of the car, but it was harder than getting in, with the steering wheel in the way. I finally made it out with a triumphant groan and turned back to get my phone, hissing out the pain as I reached across the seat to the center console.

"Got it."

I grinned like I'd accomplished something really big, but I turned and found Haynes with his gun aimed at me and froze. My grin was gone and so was any goodwill I had for the man.

When he saw my phone he holstered his gun. Did he really think I was going to unload a pistol on him?

"We'll have a uni come and get your car."

"No, you won't. I'll drive myself."

He sighed. "That's really not necessary."

"Well considering how twitchy you are, I think it is. So either I drive myself or I don't go."

The younger detective finally stepped from the car, his smarmy grin making me want to punch him in his weasel face. "You're coming with us," he insisted firmly.

I ignored him, my gaze staying on Haynes. "Am I under arrest or being detained?"

"No, we're not arresting you. We have some questions. As well as a few concerns about your safety."

"Then, I'll be right behind you." He gave a reluctant nod and tried one more time, but I brushed him off. "Someone must be dead if you're suddenly giving a shit about me."

His lack of response kept me on high alert, shaken and anxious the entire ride back to LVMPD. I was tired, sweaty and in too much pain to even contemplate things like manners and being polite. I parked on the street and stepped out, looking up at the white building. I'd rather be anywhere else than walk inside, yet I crossed the street where Haynes waited for me.

His bushy eyebrows furrowed in concern. "Are you all right?"

"You don't need to worry about me, Detective. Let's just get this over with." I followed him inside the precinct, buzzing with activity, or at least seeming to do so. They were probably letting all the calls go to voicemail and playing solitaire or on Facebook. The room was so bare and stereotypical it had to be an interrogation room. I sat gingerly on the edge of one of the hard metal chairs that had a fucking wobble.

"So what is it you want with me? I have places to go and people to see."

He sighed and waited a long minute until Detective Napoleon Complex joined us. "Where were you last night?"

"At home, where I've been for the past nine days. Recovering. And no, there's no one to confirm that." I really wished I could have crossed my arms, so I could glare at them and let both men know they didn't scare me.

"That's too bad," Dodds said and slid several pictures across the table. Pictures of a woman with stringy black hair, grey jeans and a lacy black tank top. With her face beaten and swollen the way it was, she could have been anyone. But the hummingbird tattoo between her thumb and forefinger, and the Claddagh ring on her right hand with the sapphire birthstone inside told me exactly who it was.

"Krissy. What happened to her?" I looked at Haynes because dealing with the rookie might end up with me in handcuffs.

DELICIOUSLY DAMAGED

"That's what we're trying to figure out. Anything you want to tell us?" Dodds leaned forward, smacking his hand on the lopsided metal table.

"I have a few things I'd like to tell you, little man."

He was on his feet, leaning over the table in seconds, his face red, spit flying out of his mouth as he called me every name he could think of. No matter what he said, though, he couldn't intimidate me. I barked back at him, "If this is how you treat crime victims, I'll be sure to let everyone know."

Pushing off the table with my left hand, I stood and stared down at Haynes, shaking my head.

"We both know you're no fucking victim, Mandy." He spat my name out like it left a bad taste on his tongue. "Tell us what happened and maybe you won't end up in prison for the rest of your life."

I laughed. "I'll tell you two things, Officer Dodd. One," I held up my left forefinger, "if I could swing a punch right now, it would be worth the assaulting an officer charge. Two, I'm leaving."

"I don't think so." He blocked my path and my left hand bunched and flexed, aching to knock his little ass out.

"So I'm being arrested? Great." I took a step back and smiled. "Lawyer."

Haynes groaned because I knew he'd been trying to avoid it. Cops hated when you exercised your rights. "Don't leave town, Ms. Sutton."

"Whatever. Try not to get me killed while you guys do your job, if you remember what that is."

I stared at Dodds until he moved out of my way, yanking the door open so it smacked against the painted concrete wall and marched out.

Fucking cops, useless. I made my way back to the car and fished my phone out of my purse, not easy with only one hand available to me, my other sweltering in the cast. Before I could start my car I had to make the call to the one person I knew would help without asking too many questions.

"Hey, Teddy, I need a favor."

DELICIOUSLY DAMAGED

***

Looking around the lavishly appointed office, complete with a Renoir on the walls, I felt completely out of my depth and pretty sure that this was the dumbest shit I'd ever done. I was either about to make a deal with the devil or take control of my life. What possessed me to walk into Siren Resort & Casino and demand to speak with the owner and CEO, Drake Foster, I hadn't a clue. I could blame the painkillers or the late-night staring at the mute TV in my motel room, delusions of grandeur or just plain fucking survival. But the truth was, this was it. My only shot. Two days had passed since the cops told me not to leave town and they hadn't said anything more about it.

They were no fucking help. Roadkill MC would kill me before the cops pulled their heads out of their respective asses.

"It's pretty ballsy of you to come in here like this, considering."

Drake studied me, and I studied him right back. He was a handsome guy, in a mobbed-up kind of way with dark hair he wore slicked back, beautiful skin a deep olive tone that said he spent more time on his yacht than in a windowless casino. He had big brown eyes with large flakes of gold and green, the five-thousand-dollar suit bringing the green to the forefront. But as beautiful as they were, his eyes were cold. And hard.

Yeah, considering that I'd admitted to Drake Foster that back in the day I'd counted cards in what was now his casino. "I know. I've been warned that I might end up in a shallow grave in the desert."

"Yet here you are," he said with a smile that smacked of respect even as he leaned back and crossed his legs at the ankle on one end of his desk.

"Here I am," I repeated while I gathered my words. "I decided to risk it because I was a minor at the time and using a fake I.D., which is as bad for you and the gaming commission as it is for me and the desert. Besides, I'm admitting to it because I don't do it anymore. Haven't since I left this city a decade ago."

He nodded, understanding the truth of my words. "Then why, Ms. Sutton, are you here?"

"Because I don't have a fucking choice." I sucked in a shallow breath because it was still the only thing I could manage and then told him all about Krissy and Roadkill, the debt and the tournament. "I don't really know what else to do other than keep my entry to the tournament."

Drake looked ready to throw me out of his casino right on my ass, but I kept talking. "I don't want to do this, but the cops are no help and the gang has already killed the girl who owed the money."

Why that didn't let me off the hook for this dumb shit, I didn't know. Then again, gangsters didn't really require logic to do their crimes. "I'm certain I won't win because I don't play casino games anymore but if I place, the money will go back to you or the casino, I don't care. I just have to be seen playing."

As he stared at me, I could see in his eyes he thought I was crazy or stupid. My money was on both.

"This is a dangerous game you're playing, little girl," he said assessing me before he said anything further.

I shrugged, not bothering to respond to the comment meant to rattle me. "It's dangerous either way. This way gives me a shot to live. I'm not trying to play on your sympathy, all right?"

"No?"

My laugh was harsh and bitter. "Fuck no. Not that you have any to give, but I'm not."

"Then what are you doing?" he asked, brows arched high in question.

"I'm hoping for a fucking miracle."

I didn't know what I was thinking. Maybe he'd disqualify me because of my past; it was stupid, whatever it was. I could kick myself for even thinking this could work. I had yet to meet a person I could rely on, especially those of the male persuasion. I stood, biting back the wince in my ribs just in case he thought I was trying for sympathy again. "Thanks, anyway."

"That's it? You're just giving up?" He shook his head and smacked his lips. "Guess you're not the survivor you think you are."

"Maybe not, but I do know when to cut my losses." I was disappointed but not surprised as I made my way to the door, ready to get as far from him and this place as possible.

"But you haven't lost, not yet. I have a counteroffer."

He grinned, and I braced myself for a disgusting proposition that included me on my knees and his dick in my mouth.

"I'm listening."

"My pastry chef ran off with one of my high rollers to live a life of luxury off the coast of Spain, and I have a new gourmet confectionery opening in three months. Will you be healed by then?" I shrugged and told him about the doctor's six to ten-week prognosis.

"You want the job?"

Do I want a job making gourmet sweet treats for rich mother fuckers with money to spend and a discerning palate? Fuck yeah.

"Uhm, I do."

Even though it meant I'd have to stay in Vegas, which meant letting Teddy and Jana and Savior draw me into a life filled with bikers. Bikers like Ammo, the best dude I'd ever known, but also bikers like Roadkill MC. It was a mixed bag of shit and I wasn't sure I was ready for all that.

"You might want to have a backup in case my therapy doesn't go as expected." The way my life went, it probably wouldn't.

"So we have a deal." It wasn't a question and we both knew it.

"We have a deal."

"Good, because this makes everything easier. Be here Friday at five." Before I could say another word, he picked up his phone and dialed.

Chapter 22

Savior

"What do you mean she never left town? I've spent the past week looking for Mandy from Reno to Santa Fe and now I find out she's been in Vegas the entire fucking time?" Yeah, I was pissed. "What the fuck, Teddy?"

She shrugged and flicked her red hair off her shoulders, looking like she wasn't fazed in the least. "She was on her way out of town when she was picked up by the cops on the side of the road. They wanted to talk to her about the murder of that chick who roped her into this shit. I'm surprised they haven't questioned you guys yet."

I was surprised too, but right now I had more important things to focus on, like where the hell Mandy was hiding. "So where the fuck is she?"

"She's safe. She asked for my help and I gave it to her. And I'm not giving her up unless she's in danger."

Both hands went to my head, sliding through my hair and clenching my jaws. "She is in danger, Teddy! Don't you get it?"

Golden Boy stepped between us, a dark scowl on his face as he cleared his throat. I didn't blame him. I would've done the same damn thing if it were my woman. Teddy, though, didn't seem all that amused. "Oh calm down, Tate. I can handle myself and I can definitely handle this big lug," she told him and looked at me with an arched brow. "Besides I know that men have an inability to show real emotion and this anger is worry and fear and anxiety because the woman he loves is out there and won't take his help."

"Who said I love her?" Why did women just toss the word out like they were talking about an ice-cold beer?

Her head fell back and with one hand gripping her growing belly as she laughed, like it was the funniest thing in the goddamn world.

DELICIOUSLY DAMAGED

"Are you seriously that stupid?" She held up a hand and shook her head, laughter still erupting every so often. "I guess so. Well then, since you don't love her then you should trust me when I tell you she's fine."

"She's not!" I roared at her and the fact that she didn't even flinch pissed me off and impressed me. "Roadkill MC is after her. They've already killed Krissy; do you think they'll hesitate to do the same to her when they find her?"

I couldn't even think about that shit. If they touched one hair on her head, I'd be forced to become the man I hadn't been in years. The stone-cold killer who'd do whatever it took to protect his brothers. Both in the sandbox and here at home.

"Because you're the only one who could possibly keep her safe, right?" One long pink fingernail poked me in my chest. "For your information, I paid for her room and she has a new car, which is why you, Mr. Nosy Butt, saw her old one at the car lot."

When she was done yelling at me, Teddy stepped back and crossed her arms, waiting for me to say something.

"Tell me where she is, Teddy."

"No. She's my friend and she called me, not you. If she wants to see you, she'll let me know and I won't tell you a minute before."

Damn, I couldn't help but smile at her loyalty. Mandy thought she didn't have anyone left who gave a damn about her, but she did. Teddy was as feisty as a mama bear protecting her cubs.

"Don't smile at me like that, you piss me off," she snarled, trying to hide a grin.

"I know I do, and you should be, but I still need to know where she is."

"Because you love her?"

I groaned and palmed my face. "Really, Teddy? Right now?"

She flashed that cover girl smile and pressed a kiss to my cheek. "Good luck."

"Damn, you're seriously not gonna tell me?"

"Nope."

"Thanks for nothing, Cover Girl." I winked at her shocked gasp and left, phone in hand to call the Reckless Bastards' resident computer geek.

"Jag, I need your help." I waited until I was out of hearing distance before I asked for this particular favor, knowing if I was Golden Boy, I wouldn't appreciate it either.

"I need you to track Teddy's credit cards. See which hotel she's paying for."

"Everything all right, man?"

"Fuck no, man. Mandy is still here in town and I need to find her. Now." I could hear Jag's fingers already flying over the keyboard.

"Fine, but when Golden Boy finds out, I expect you to have my back."

I laughed because we both knew Jag was a certified badass with weapons and hand-to-hand combat, never mind his computer skills and GB would never find out.

"I'll handle it," I promised.

"All right. Keep your phone on, I'll have something for you soon."

Finally, one goddamn thing was going my way.

***

Teddy, that little liar, made me waste a full day searching for Mandy when she knew damn well she hadn't paid for the hotel room, or if she had, it was in a different name other than her own. Driving around Vegas at night was a bitch. Pedestrian traffic meant everything took twice as long and by the time either me or Jag realized it, night had come and gone.

DELICIOUSLY DAMAGED

Imagine my surprise when I was strolling down the Vegas Strip, trying to see where she might have gone, when I got a text from Teddy with just one word.

"Siren."

I smiled and doubled back, making my way to the newest casino to hit the strip. My footsteps faltered for a minute as all the pieces settled into my brain. Siren was hosting the blackjack tournament. Tonight. My speed doubled and it doubled again, my feet carrying me closer toward Mandy. Toward the casino where Roadkill MC was waiting to collect their earnings. Over my dead fucking body.

Once I made my way across the blue and green lobby, decked out to look like the sea with elaborate paintings of the sirens the place was name after, and through the clang and ding of the slot machines, the roar of wins at the table games, I finally spotted it. The bright lights, cameras and the hustle and bustle gave away the back room location of the blackjack tournament. Apparently, it was being televised. I didn't know how the thugs convinced her to do this, but it must be serious.

I spotted Mandy talking with some slick asshole in a suit, his hand on her shoulder like he had a fucking right to touch her. She was my woman, goddammit. My hands itched to rip him away from her and pound his face until my knuckles bled. But she didn't shrug him off or even look upset, so I stayed back. Far enough so she didn't feel like I was interfering but close enough to jump in if I needed to.

The first thing I noticed was that she'd cut her cast back. Now it only covered her wrist so that her hand was free. She wore a top with long sleeves and if you didn't know about her injuries, you might miss it. Her therapy must be going well, I thought. Shit. I'd fucking know that if she'd let me into her life.

"Sir, stay back please." A big ass bald dude in all black blocked my view.

"Sorry. That's my girl and I just wanted to make sure she knew I was here. For luck, ya know?" I flashed a friendly smile and the man nodded.

DELICIOUSLY DAMAGED

"Understood, but security is tight tonight."

Thank fuck for that shit. I looked around, hoping to spot members of Roadkill MC but if they were here, they were well hidden. I did see my own family, though, Jana with Max and Teddy and Golden Boy. Beside them sat Cross, Lasso and Stitch. I didn't know the woman with long black hair streaked with grey sitting between Stitch and Jag. I couldn't help but smile at all the people who'd shown up for Mandy. She might not know they were there, but if she did, it would mean a lot to the woman who still believed she was all alone in this world.

She didn't know how wrong she was.

I took a seat at the end of the row beside Jag, watching Mandy. As she played, her gaze fixed on nothing but the cards, hers and the dealer, tapping the table or shoving her cards away.

The tournament began with twenty tables but as they dwindled down, the local news anchor and former blackjack champion hosting the event, went around to each table talking softly behind the players explaining what was happening. As the hours flew by, the tables went from twenty to twelve to seven and finally down to two. The action was surprisingly tense considering how fucking boring the game of blackjack was, with bets getting bigger, players getting bolder and a few even talking smack to each other.

"Okay folks," Wendy Crewson, the attractive anchorwoman broke in. "We now have our final table. After a quick break, we'll get started on the final action!"

Wendy smiled at the camera and when the director yelled "Cut!" the slick asshole I'd seen with Mandy when I first arrived came out with a woman in a crisp skirt suit and a clipboard.

He leaned in to whisper in Wendy's ear, his hand on her lower back. Apparently the guy just liked to rub his paws all over women. Slick Asshole pulled back and gave a solemn nod before they both approached . . . Mandy.

Shit.

DELICIOUSLY DAMAGED

They pulled her aside into a huddle, talking quietly for a few minutes before they pulled apart. Mandy's expression was impassive, her hands clasped in front of her as she stood between the suit and the newswoman.

"And we're back!" The director pointed to Wendy with her anchorwoman smile fixed on her face.

"We're back for the First Annual Siren Blackjack Tournament and a little bit of excitement has gone down on our break. We have the disqualification of a player and Siren owner and CEO Drake Foster is here to explain."

Slick Asshole was disqualifying her? What the fuck?

"Thank you, Wendy, that's right. It's come to my attention that Mandy will be our new chef at the gourmet confectionery that will open in a few months. The Chocolate Drop will be the best place for high end sweets in all of Las Vegas, just as soon as Mandy here has recovered from some injuries." He wrapped an arm around Mandy, who gave him a shaky smile. "Though her employment here hasn't technically started, management and I agree that for the sake of fairness, it would be best if she withdrew from the tournament. Sorry, Mandy. We don't want to give the appearance of a conflict of interest."

He smiled and handed his mic back to Wendy before escorting Mandy away from the final table.

I needed to know what the fuck was going on. I followed them down the hall, surprised when no big ass security men tackled me to the ground.

"Mandy!" She stopped and turned. Slick Asshole did the same. She looked relieved while he looked anxious as my stride ate up the distance between us. I cupped her face in my hands, looking into those green eyes just to make sure she was all right.

"You scared the hell out of me! Don't ever do that again," I told her and yanked her into my arms, holding her tight until I was sure she was safe.

"Everything okay here, Mandy?" His skin paled under that fake ass spray tan when I glared at him.

I was about to tell the asshole to fuck off when another voice sounded.

"Yo, Mandy!" The tension I felt snaking through her told me it was trouble before I turned and spotted a Roadkill mother fucker I was familiar with. Scorch.

"Stay back," I growled at them both, pushing Mandy directly behind me.

"I have security," Slick Asshole said, a tremble of fear in his voice.

"Yeah, where the fuck are they, then?"

I kept my attention on Scorch, enforcer for Roadkill MC and a sick fucker who got off on hurting people. "Scorch, don't be stupid."

He smiled. "This ain't about you or the Reckless Bastards, Savior. We want the bitch, she owes us."

"I don't owe you shit," she shouted over my shoulder. That was my girl, feisty as ever.

"You heard the lady, man. Don't make me do something you might regret."

Scorch tossed his head back and laughed, running a hand through his hair in an attempt to prove he wasn't scared, but he was. Because while Scorch was a psychopath, he knew I was a fucking killer.

"You can't protect the bitch forever. She has a debt to pay, cash or ass."

"You willing to bet your life that I can't protect her forever?"

"Savior, don't," Mandy whispered in my ear, fueling my intensity to protect her.

"You willing to bet your life for a piece of ass?" Scorch laughed like it was the biggest joke in the world and it took every fucking ounce of control I had not to charge him and choke him until he was permanently silent.

I smiled a deadly smile that had made more than one grown man piss his pants. "Damn straight I am. Have you seen my girl's sweet ass? If you had a brain you'd leave now, before the security goons and the law shows up."

DELICIOUSLY DAMAGED

I backed Mandy up and punched the call button on the elevator because this asshole wouldn't stop. The debt Krissy owed was big enough that he'd risk the life of a few of his brothers to get it back.

"I texted Teddy our location," she whispered, hands on my shoulders, keeping me calm even though she didn't know it. I couldn't be reckless, not with Mandy so close to the line of fire.

My hand reached out to pat her hip. "That's my girl."

"You keep saying that," she said and I heard the smile in her voice.

"It's true," I told her as my other hand went to my hip, pulling out my Glock. "So what's it gonna be, Scorch, life or death?" The bell sounded, and I shoved Mandy into the elevator and then Slick Asshole.

"Ow!" Mandy's cry drew my attention at the most inopportune moment, but I had to make sure she was all right. I called out, "Mandy, you okay? Shit!"

The sound of the gun firing came too late, and a bullet went sailing right through my shoulder. "Motherfucker!" I fired off three shots, hitting one of the assholes next to Scorch before I jumped in the elevator.

"See what happens when you put your life on the line for a piece of ass?" His voice drew closer and I kept my gun trained on the doors, which were still fucking closing.

"Door!" I shouted at Slick Asshole, who seemed to be frozen in fear. "The goddamn door!"

Finally, he jumped into action and pressed the close button just as Scorch and one of his men stood in front of the closing doors. I fired three shots as the car began to move. "Holy shit! What the fuck?" Slick Asshole stared at Mandy, eyes wide with terror.

"Two dead assholes," I told him and then collapsed to the floor of the elevator. I'd been shot before, a few flesh wounds and one that ripped through my stomach years ago, so I knew the deal, but I was losing blood fast.

"Savior! Shit, you're hurt." She cupped my face and I knew what she saw, my eyes glassy and dazed. Her eyes missed nothing, staring at my shoulder spurting blood. "Jacket," she barked at the man, snapping her fingers and I had to smile. Mandy was still trying to control the uncontrollable. "Shirt too," she said distractedly.

"This suit costs—"

"Give me the fucking clothes!"

If I wasn't in so much pain and losing blood like I had any to spare, I would have laughed at how quickly Slick Asshole removed his jacket and then his button-up shirt.

"Here," he shoved his jacket at Mandy and watched as she folded it and put it under my head, then the expensive silk blue shirt.

She snapped her fingers again and pointed to his bony chest. He got it, peeling off his wife beater and handing it to her with shaky hands. Shock. Despite his mobster look, the guy was probably an Ivy Leaguer who'd never even heard a gunshot outside of TV.

"Thank you, Drake." She balled up the t-shirt and pressed it to my shoulder, pulling a string of colorful curses from me. "Sorry, but we have to stop the bleeding."

"I know. You worried about me, Pixie?" My smile was weak, but her lips curved in response.

Then turned into a glare. "You took a bullet for me dumbass, of course I am." Her expression softened, eyes the color of jade flickered with worry and maybe even affection.

Despite the pressure, the elevator floor was more red than blue at this point as blood spurted out of my shoulder. It was probably an artery, I thought as black spots clouded my vision.

"Aww, Mandy, I love you too." At least I thought that was what I said to her, but what the hell did I know?

Chapter 23

Mandy

My heart never pounded so much in my entire life as it did when I watched Savior's big strong body crumple to the floor in a bloody heap. Having him passed out in my arms might have induced a heart attack, but I couldn't move my hands, not with the way the blood spurted out. I didn't know much about wounds, but in culinary school we'd all had our fair share of cuts so I knew the first key was to stop the bleeding.

One look at Drake and I wanted to scream, but his back was to me while he whispered into the phone. I wondered who he could possibly be talking to at a time like this, but I didn't say anything. It wasn't my place. I was just a future employee. Drake ended his call and pocketed his phone before turning to me with a frown. "We have a concierge doctor on staff, he's meeting us in the penthouse suite."

"Thanks, Drake. Sorry about all this, and I can pay for the suit." My voice wobbled in relief. There was no way Savior would make it even if we got him to a car right now, not in Vegas traffic. The hospital was an easy twenty minutes away on a good night.

"You can pay for the suit?"

I understood his question even as I ignored his incredulous tone.

"A lifetime of dead family members will do that," I told him, my gaze still on Savior, whose pulse had slowed enough that my own heart lurched into my stomach.

"Shit. Tough girl."

I shrugged. I wasn't tough. No, I was numb and hollow. Too much loss and not enough of anything else.

"Life demands it. Look Drake, I'm sorry about all this and I completely get it if you want to rescind the job offer."

He frowned, his hazel eyes sparking gold against the mirrored walls of the elevator. "You kidding me?

DELICIOUSLY DAMAGED

Your boyfriend saved my life. The job is still yours, if you're not traumatized every time you come to work." His hand shook as it scraped through his dark hair, which wasn't as perfectly coifed as it had been earlier.

I nodded at his words, but I couldn't focus on him when Savior was unconscious and bleeding. "Come on, Savior, wake up! Say something dirty or stupid or piss me off! Please!" I leaned over and touched my forehead to his, feeling something in my heart crack wide open at the sight of him lying there. Lifeless. I couldn't lose him.

"I never would have pegged you to date a biker." Drake's words drifted down, disbelief coloring his words.

"I'm not. We're not dating, not really." Hell, I hadn't seen Savior in at least a week and I'd been fully prepared to leave town without a goodbye.

"The man took a bullet for you and said he loved you, so maybe between physical therapy and playing nurse to him, you might want to figure your shit out."

At my incredulous look, he shrugged. "I need you one hundred percent when you start, and a confectioner in love will make me plenty of money."

I couldn't help the bark of laughter that escaped. "Your concern is overwhelming."

"Thanks. I'll try to tamp it down."

The doors finally slid open at the penthouse and I looked down at Savior again, limp and lifeless. "Vick! Wake up." I tapped his cheek lightly, silently pleading with him to come to. There was no way Drake and I could carry him even a few feet.

"Savior," I practically shouted. His lips curled at the corners first and then those big blue eyes fluttered open and I swear, my heart straight up sighed. "There you are," I said on a whisper. "I need you to stand up so we can get you to the doctor."

His face, already twisted in pain, turned hard. "No fucking hospital."

I rolled my eyes. "Stubborn ass. My new boss has a fancy doctor on staff, so just get on your damn feet and lean on us so we can get you looked at."

I handed Drake his jacket. He put it on, smoothing it down over his bare chest.

Savior blinked and nodded, grunting as Drake and I helped him to his feet. "Where the hell was your security, uhm …"

"Drake," he filled in for him. "And I've got someone looking into just that now. Thanks for that."

Savior grunted as we got him into the suite and onto the bed. The doctor, a bald man in a nice blue suit and crisp brown eyes, helped us get him on the bed. While the doctor looked him over, I pulled out my phone, trying to figure out who to call. Savior's grasp tightened on my hand and I looked down at him with a smile.

"Take it easy, cowboy, I'm just telling everyone you're all right." His grip didn't loosen and I stood there beside him. I could tell them later. Right now, I was just glad Savior was okay.

The doctor cut his long sleeve t-shirt off and examined the wound, drawing a wince from Savior. He turned to me. "Can you grab some towels? I need to flush this out." Then he started preparing a bunch of medical stuff and I gave Savior's hand one last squeeze before leaving the room.

All I could think about as I grabbed two handfuls of fluffy white towels from the bathroom was that Savior had taken a bullet for me. He'd come to watch out for me, maybe even to support me and I'd been an insensitive asshole for the past few weeks. He said he loved me and I wanted to believe him. I wasn't sure I believed in love, didn't even know if I could love after losing my brother, but my heart wanted to believe Savior loved me.

Which meant I was totally fucking screwed.

Because I loved him too. The way my heart stopped when he collapsed, the bone deep ache in my stomach from missing him, had been trying to tell me what I was determined to ignore. That despite my insistence, my better judgment and my hardened heart, I'd fallen in love with a biker. A soldier.

"I can feel you staring at me, Pixie. Get your sweet ass in here."

I didn't know how he knew I was there, watching him but I didn't care. I needed to be near him.

And when I was, I couldn't stop touching him, assuring myself that he was okay while the doctor arranged the towels underneath him. "I'm glad you're all right."

"Thanks to you, Pixie."

The doctor cleared his throat. "It's a through and through and I've cleaned and bandaged it up. I have some painkillers and antibiotics I can give you now, as well as prescriptions for later."

He gave a few care instructions and left his card, before leaving us alone in the suite. Drake had already left, probably to fire his security team, if I had to make a guess. Probably grabbing a shirt before he chewed someone's ass.

"I guess I'm going to have to take care of you." The idea of that didn't sound so bad.

"Yeah? Where you gonna do that, Pixie, your mysterious hotel room?"

My shoulders deflated at his words. He was right. I had a job and until that one started, a temporary job taking care of Savior. And no place to live.

"Don't you worry about that, I can take care of you and look for a place to live."

He shook his head, clasping our hands together. "No need. My place is big enough for two."

"I'm not moving in with you," I told him, smiling against his lips before sealing them together in a kiss that was both tender and thrilling. Sweet and hot. He winced and that was my cue to pull back, still smiling.

"I meant it, you know, Pixie. I do love you."

DELICIOUSLY DAMAGED

Tears pooled in my eyes and I felt like one of those silly women who got all choked up at the barest hint of affection, but I could tell behind the pain and behind his own fear of saying such significant words, that he meant it. He really did love me. But it wasn't something I could handle right now. I believed him, but tonight had been ... a lot. I kissed him softly and pulled back. "Tell me again when you haven't lost a few gallons of blood."

"Don't worry ... I ... will," he said, smiling sleepily before he passed out.

I smiled and sat beside him, holding his hand and watching him sleep for hours. This, me and Savior, was something special. And scary as hell. But as I sat there, letting the slow rise and fall of his sleeping form soothe my frazzled nerves, I knew I wouldn't run away from it again. Things might end badly, and they probably would if history was any indication, but I had a feeling it would be amazing in the meantime.

But first, I needed to clean all this blood off of me.

KB WINTERS

Epilogue

Six months. Savior and I had been living together for six months and it hadn't turned bad. I was even starting to believe that it might not. Which was cause for celebration.

Today was supposed to be my day off but I'd spent a few hours in the morning checking over the chocolates I'd ordered from South America and putting together a few gourmet baskets I wanted to test out in the shop. I dropped one off for Drake and took the others to Jana and Teddy, who'd had their babies eight weeks apart. Visiting with them, watching two new mothers fall in love with their children was gratifying. And it solidified what I wanted to do today.

What I *needed* to do.

When I got home, I took a long hot shower and set the scene. I didn't want Jana and Teddy to make a big deal out of it, so I stopped at a craft store on the way home and got everything I needed. It took a few minutes to get everything in place, but when it was, I got dolled up and slipped into the only pair of stilettos I owned. And then I waited for Savior to get home from the clubhouse.

At least he wasn't on one of those mysterious out of town trips they took every other month. I didn't ask and didn't want to know, but I always felt happy relief when he came back to me. Safe and smiling.

"Pixie?"

I smiled at the sound of his deep voice and that damned nickname he insisted on calling me. "In here," I called to him when I stepped out of the bathroom attached to our bedroom, my heart double palpitating in my chest as his footsteps grew closer. I didn't think he'd reject me but still I felt anxious. Terrified.

His footsteps stopped in the doorway and his lips parted slightly, blue eyes turned as dark as the desert night sky. "You trying to kill me, babe?"

My heart lifted right along with my lips at his words, his gritty tone filled with need. "Not at all, I'm trying to seduce you."

We both really needed a proper seduction after six months of injuries, with healing and physical therapy we'd only had a few clumsy attempts at getting off. "Is it working?"

He stepped forward, hand gripping his thick cock and he quirked a brow, smiling beneath his newly trimmed beard. "What do you think?"

I couldn't resist brushing his hand aside and gripping him in my fist. And squeezing. "I think my mouth is watering."

"And I think ribbons are my new favorite fucking thing." His eyes raked over my body, confirming that all the time I'd spent wrapping the thick satiny ribbon around my body in a peekaboo pattern, was totally worth it. "Come here."

I shook my head and his hands shot to my waist, pulling me close and kissing my neck. Big, warm hands slid up and down my body, stoking the fire that had been burning since I wrapped myself up for him. "Savior," I moaned, nipping at the muscle between his shoulder and neck.

"I can't believe you did this. For me?" His eyes filled with awe and a hell of a lot of heat as I nodded and cupped his face, letting my fingers slide through his beard.

"I figured this and that memory was the best place to start." That day on the water had seemed like such an anomaly, a rare genuinely happy day, but in hindsight it was when he started working his magic, tearing down my walls.

"For what?" The heat was still there, banked, but also concern. I wasn't worried because I knew it would soon be gone. "For what, Pixie?"

I pressed my lips to his, smiling when his hand found one edge of the ribbon and tugged, groaning when I stepped back. "To tell you that I love you. You're insane and you're brash, short tempered and so overprotective that I want to bite you and not in a sexy way."

"You could have stopped at 'I love you'." He sounded grumpy.

I rolled my eyes and scraped my nails along his bearded jaw, drawing a low purr from him. "I wasn't sure I could love anyone anymore, thought my heart was too battered and broken for that, but you found a way in and I think it started with that day on the water. Laughing together, forgetting all the shit even just for a few hours. I love you, Savior."

"Again," he growled.

"I. Love. You." I slid my hands under the hem of his t-shirt, letting my hands glide up his hard abs and chest. "I know it took me forever to say it," I smiled sheepishly.

"Pretty damn close," he mumbled.

"But I had to wait until I was ready. Until we were ready and I could say it. Today is that day."

He kissed my mouth, my neck and my shoulder, his words from San Diego echoing in my mind. He slowly unraveled the ribbon, putting kisses everywhere the ribbon uncovered. "Ah, sweet Pixie. I love you too, babe and hearing you finally say it, fuck, I just want to spend the rest of the day worshipping you."

"Mmm, sounds good to me." My head tilted back and I smiled.

He cupped my face, his gaze intense and filled with pure love. "You're mine, Mandy. I'm yours. And I'm keeping you forever. How does that sound?"

I smiled and licked my lips, feeling my heart swell bigger than it had ever felt before. "Fan-fucking-tastic."

* * * *

~ THE END ~

Acknowledgements

Thank you so much for making my books a success! I appreciate all of you! Thanks to all of my beta readers, street teamers, ARC readers and Facebook fans. Y'all are THE BEST!

And a huge very special thanks to Jessie! I'm such a *hot mess, but without your keen sense of organization and skills, I'd be a burny fiery inferno of hot mess!! Thank you!

And a very special thanks to my editors (who sometimes have to work all through the night! *See HOT MESS above!) Thank you for making my words make sense.

Copyright © 2018 KB Winters and BookBoyfriends Publishing LLC

KB WINTERS

About The Author

KB Winters is a Wall Street Journal and USA Today Bestselling Author of steamy hot books about Bikers, Billionaires, Bad Boys and Badass Military Men. Just the way you like them. She has an addiction to caffeine, tattoos and hard-bodied alpha males. The men in her books are very sexy, protective and sometimes bossy, her ladies are…well…*bossier*!

Living in sunny Southern California, with her five kids and three fur babies, this embarrassingly hopeless romantic writes every chance she gets!

You can reach me at Facebook.com/kbwintersauthor and at kbwintersauthor@gmail.com

Copyright © 2018 KB Winters and BookBoyfriends Publishing LLC

Printed in Great Britain
by Amazon